Father God it Hurts

Trusting God When Bad Things Happen

Frank Angerillo

Father God It Hurts

Stratton Press Publishing
831 N Tatnall Street Suite M #188,
Wilmington, DE 19801
www.stratton-press.com
1-888-323-7009

ISBN (Paperback): 978-1-64345-540-2
ISBN (Hardback): 978-1-64345-724-6
ISBN (Ebook): 978-1-64345-655-3

Printed in the United States of America

Contents

Introduction

Every day, bad things happen in the world and to good people, and no one can explain why. Religious leaders have different views concerning bad events and evil in the world. Many of these views concern God and whether he has the power to prevent bad things from happening. This book outlines the factors behind bad events and evil in the world.

There are many factors to consider when something bad happens to us or a loved one. The only question is what factor caused the event. Often, people want to blame God when bad things happen to them. Yet they ignore the power and influence that Satan has in the world. Although Satan is not omnipresent, he has many demons assigned to individuals and nations. This legion of evil is responsible for many of the bad things that occur in the world.

In addition, our choices and free will are factors to consider when bad things happen to us. God put in place natural and biblical laws for us to follow. When we reject these laws, bad consequences can follow. Yet despite our bad decisions, God is ready to heal our wounds once we place our trust and hope in him.

Another factor that is often overlooked when bad events occur is random chance. Yet this factor is responsible for many of the bad things we experience in life. Furthermore, often we blame God or the devil for random, chance bad events. In view of this, the believer should always exercise discernment before casting blame on the devil or God for a bad event. Likewise, conceding all things to God is the key for enduring trials in this world.

Chapter 1

WHY

Every day, terrible things happen in the world, and people want to know why. When young innocent children are gunned down at school, the event shocks us. As a result, the political opinions from the Left and Right are voiced. The Left blames the attack on one's violent upbringing and their mental health condition, whereas the Right contends it's their parents' fault and lack of accountability by society. Even though both views have valid points, neither side concedes ground to the other. Thus, agreeing on measures to prevent future attacks are never implemented.

A massive tornado hits Oklahoma City, and hundreds of homes are destroyed. Thousands of people are left homeless and financially devastated. People demand immediate assistance from their politicians, but the relief effort is slow in coming. Thereafter, the positions of the Left and Right are voiced. The Left will contend it's the government fault for not investing in early detection equipment, whereas the Right will proclaim that people knew the risks associated with living in tornado alley; therefore, the government is not responsible for their losses. Likewise, religion is brought into the conversation. Religious leaders claim it's God wrath on a sinful nation while others don't believe a loving God would allow such a terrible thing to happen.

Your pastor receives a call from the doctor's office concerning his test results. The receptionist says the doctor would like to see him and his spouse tomorrow at 9:00 a.m. So he is concerned, but not overly anxious. He thinks it's just high cholesterol or some other test result his wife should keep an eye on. The next morning when he walks into the office, the doctor says those dreaded words: "I am sorry, but I am afraid that I have some bad news for you." Immediately his wife starts crying, and fear totally grips him. He has an inoperable brain tumor and has six months to live.

After the initial fear subsides, he starts the why questions: "Why me? Why, God? This cannot be happening to me because I am a pastor. Who is going to take care of my family?" In time, he accepts his fate. But he questions his faith in God and whether he is all-powerful. After all, he is a good person who is serving the Lord, and bad things like this only happen to bad people. Likewise, his wife questions her faith too because her husband is the financial provider. Thus, she is worried about her future.

You are watching a documentary concerning the plight of India's 900 million impoverished people. When they explain about the caste system in India, you rightly reject it as something that is morally wrong. The people should resist and change this ignorant system, you think, but they don't. Moreover, the people in India accept the caste system because Hindus accept their lot in life. Again, you think to yourself, why would anybody believe such nonsense? Later that evening, you watch a news report about teenagers joining ISIS to fight the Americans. They interview one of the ISIS teenagers. He says dying for the cause of Allah is his goal. You are troubled by this teenager's fanatical views.

These types of bad scenarios occur every day in our world, and no one can explain why. Everyone has their theories and opinions as to why bad things happen in the world. Some contend people can avoid bad things by making good choices in life, while others believe luck and missed opportunities are the reasons why bad things happen to good people. Although there are many opinions concerning why bad events occur in the world, one's culture shapes the way they view tragedy and loss in the world. This extends to one's opinion of God too.

When bad things happen to good people, God often gets the blame. Many people want to know why God won't stop bad things from happening in the world. Religious leaders in the world have different views on the matter. Some religions believe that everything is God's will. So you accept your fate in life and stop complaining. Conversely, some religions believe it's God will, but through good works, your fate and fortune can change. Other religions believe there is a God, but he is powerless to stop bad things from happening. Because of all the conflicting religious dogma in the world, many people question whether there is a God.

There are many religious books in the world that offer insight about evil in the world. The Bible is the most popular and widely read religious book in the world. There are sixty-six books within the Bible: thirty-nine in the Old Testament and twenty-seven in the New Testament. The Bible was written over a 1,500-year period by forty different authors. Although the Bible's theme is God's relationship with mankind, there are other spiritual messages too, messages pertaining to morality, obedience, faith, and spiritual warfare between angels and demons.

We find in the book of Genesis verses that imply that mankind has great potential. We find this statement in Genesis 11:5–8: "But the Lord came down to see the city and tower which the sons of men had built. And the Lord said, 'Indeed the people are one and they all have one language, and this is what they begin to do; now nothing that they propose to do will be withheld from them. Come, let Us go down and there confuse their language, that they may not understand one another's speech.'" In view of this passage, some believe God created mankind with the ability to foresee and prevent bad things from happening in the world.

MANKIND

Mankind has achieved unparalleled knowledge in every field of study in this century. The breakthroughs in the fields of technology, natural laws, environmental science, and astronomy are unprecedented. Likewise, our understanding of human behavior through the fields of psychology and sociology have improved the quality of life for millions. In view of the advancements in these fields, it may be possible to devise contingency models that can anticipate bad events by weighing factors since models are already used in the fields of science, engineering, and mathematics.

To devise models that can forecast events in the world, identifying known factors is necessary. Take for instance our daily commute to work every morning. The known factors to consider are traffic, weather conditions, and accidents—they can all impact when you arrive at work. In addition, there are unlikely factors to consider such as mechanic problems with your car, your involvement in an accident, or a family emergency. Any one of these factors or a combination of them can affect your daily commute.

If something as mundane as driving to work every day has known factors that can be measured and forecast results, then it might be possible to predict complex scenarios too. This can be done by knowing what factors to weigh for given situations. Furthermore, factors can be arranged into categories. For example, the known factors for our drive-to-work scenario would fall under the probability or chance category. In view of this, it might be possible to analyze factors within categories and develop models that can predict results.

All models are based on factors that predict outcomes. However, if you change factors within models, your outcomes will change too. Hence, there is a cause-and-effect principle at work here. Furthermore, the basis for the models are logic, science, and mathematics. So if we plug in these rational laws into models, we get probability outcomes. Conversely, when we plug in supernatural factors into models, the outcomes are no longer predictable. Thus, supernatural factors like God, Satan, and human nature can change predictable outcomes in models.

PROBABILITY OR CHANCE CATEGORY

Few people view probability or chance as a mathematical factor that can predict outcomes when in fact, several businesses rely on and base their industry on them. For example, the gambling industry across the country generates millions through state lotteries and casinos. These state lotteries seldom shut down for lack of revenue. Likewise, barring mismanagement or recessions, few casinos lose money. They don't lose money because the factor of probability or chance favors the casino. Unfortunately, few gamblers would argue otherwise.

Most people would agree that gambling is a game of chance. Chance or probability is a factor in gambling that can be measured mathematically. For example, if you're playing blackjack against the dealer, the number of players in the game determines the probabilities of the cards dealt. Hence, the house dealer has an advantage over the players due to his experience because he knows the probabilities in each game based on the cards played. Although people like to believe in luck when they win a hand, the truth is they won because of the law of probability.

When I worked as an insurance agent in the eighties, I was informed that it took fifteen months before an auto policy earned money for the company. Hence, insurance agents had to be aggressive in selling life, home, and other products to earn higher salaries and make profits for their company. This fifteen-month threshold was based on the law of probability. In view of this law, insurance companies could project the number of auto accidents annually based on historical data. This data coupled with the number of new policies annually provided the factors necessary to project profitability time frames.

The entire insurance industry is based on given probabilities and factors. Take for example the number of car accidents you've experienced in your lifetime. Think about the factors that caused these accidents; your age, miles driven daily, large city versus small-town employment, weather conditions, and drunk drivers all played a role in these accidents. In view of these factors, could you have done anything differently to avoid them? In addition, your insurance company knew based on probability that most people will experience seven car accidents in their lifetime—two of which will be serious.

On a personal note, I lived in Minnesota until I was nineteen, so I knew a lot about driving during the winter. Since leaving Minnesota, I have been involved in two winter accidents. And despite my cold-weather driving experience, it didn't preclude me from these two accidents. Although I didn't panic and make matters worse after losing control of my vehicle, I didn't blame anyone or proclaimed that God, the devil, or bad karma were responsible for these accidents. I knew then and now these accidents occurred because of the weather conditions.

In the Bible, Jesus seems to suggest that random chance occurs, whether people are good or bad. We find this suggestion in Luke 13:4–5: "Or those eighteen on whom the tower in Siloam fell and killed them, do you think that they were worse sinners than all other men who dwelt in Jerusalem? I tell you, no; but unless you repent you will all likewise perish."

Although Jesus was speaking of salvation and repentance in these verses, he is also stating that bad things can happen to people by chance.

Often when people lose loved ones in automobile accidents, they want to blame others or want to know why. Granted, family members of victims due to a DUI (driving under the influence) driver have a person to blame. However, did that accident occur because of divine judgment or an evil presence? The short answer is no because in most vehicle accidents, there are known factors that caused them.

For example, in the state of Missouri, drunk drivers are responsible for 30 percent of the automobile accidents in the state. That 30 percent is a probability factor that has nothing to do with God, the devil, or karma. In view of this, if you're involved in a car accident in Missouri, there is a 30 percent chance the driver responsible for it was drunk. If so, there is an increase probability that someone may get killed or maimed in that accident.

I contend the law of probability or chance does not discriminate. It applies to the good, bad, and indifferent people of the world. In view of this, whenever a good person is killed or maimed in a car accident, there are measurable factors behind it. Although we may want to believe in some hidden force behind an accident, perhaps the only reason for it was due to the law of chance or probability.

Although this explanation may seem unfair or unacceptable to us, it's based on the law of probability or chance.

If probability and chance is a law based on mathematics, then how or who created it? There are two possible explanations for its creation: it was either created by an all-powerful God or by natural forces that formed after the creation of the universe. One could present evidence to support either position. Conversely, one could argue the validity against either position. In view of this, how one views the law of probability or chance is how they understand the forces that created the universe.

In the Bible, we find a passage that supports the law of probability or chance. King Solomon is the writer of this passage. He contends there is nothing we can do to change our fate. We find this in Ecclesiastes 9:11–12: "I returned and saw under the sun that—The race is not to the swift, Nor the battle to the strong, Nor bread to the wise, Nor riches to men of understanding, Nor favor to men of skill; But time and chance happen to them all. For man also does not know his time: Like fish taken in a cruel net, Like birds caught in a snare, So the sons of men are snared in an evil time, When it falls suddenly upon them."

ENVIRONMENT/CULTURE/UPBRINGING CATEGORY

Few would dispute that one's environment and upbringing determines their success or failure in life. The racial unrest in the United States confirms this point. The people in these troubled communities have little hope for the future. They have little hope because of all the negative forces within their environment. An environment in which they have seen, been taught, and experienced unfair treatment by those in authority. This perception coupled with limited opportunities for a better life has caused real anger and resentment within these communities. Hence, one bad confrontation with the police can trigger a riot in these areas.

The factors of poverty, poor education, limited job opportunities, and rampant crime and drugs are formidable obstacles that few overcome. Granted, many poor kids through athletics escape their environment. Likewise, some urban kids beat the odds and achieve success through academics. Many poor kids, however, are not great athletes, nor are they strong students. Therefore, their options are limited. This factor coupled with the violence within these communities scar many young people. Furthermore, many teens get killed or injured due to the gang violence in these areas.

Another factor that is often overlooked concerning those who live in the inner city: low expectations and self-esteem. We are a by-product of our environment and the people in our lives. Therefore, the importance of education and hard work means little to those with no role models to emulate. On a personal note, I grew up in Minnesota, and my family was poor until I entered the eighth grade. Likewise, neither my father nor mother attended college. These factors coupled with my struggles in school because of my ADD (attention deficit disorder) negatively affected my self-esteem. Thus, I never considered college after high school because in my opinion, I was not smart enough to attend. So if I had not joined the military after high school, neither my environment nor expectations would have changed.

In contrast, poor people in Third World countries have no chance for a better life because people living in the Third World with intelligence, talent, or athletic abilities are not guaranteed anything. In view of this, the principles of hard work, perseverance, drive, determination, and confidence necessary for success in the Western World means nothing to those trapped by Third World poverty. That reality is difficult for Americans to accept.

FAMILY

Even though there are serious problems in the United States concerning race and income disparity, these problems are solvable with education and employment opportunities. In view of this, poor children born in the United States can still achieve success in life. Moreover, a child's chances for success improves greatly with the love and support from one or two parents because family structure and support matters. And this support can motivate people to overcome the negative factors of poverty.

Family structure in the United States has changed significantly since the fifties. But what has not changed is the importance that parents and mentors play in nurturing children. So regardless of one's political persuasion or religious beliefs, they would agree that children must be taught to do the right things. Thus, what children are taught can affect their entire life. In addition, children must be taught and believe that they can achieve goals despite their environment. In short, one's upbringing matters. Likewise, that upbringing is not always where a child lives, but the support they receive within their home and extended community.

Americans believe in fairness. They also believe that a person who is intelligent and works hard can overcome anything—even if they live in a bad environment. In principle, there is truth to that statement. Yet without strong support from family and mentors, most children fail to overcome the forces of poverty. Conversely, poor children born in the Third World with good upbringings still fail to achieve success in life, mainly because the opportunities available to children in the United States are not available to those living in Third World countries. This is not a matter of fairness, but one of geography and fate.

There is no doubt that one's environment, culture, and upbringing shape them. Likewise, there is a tendency for those born in the United States to judge or belittle the plight of those born in the Third World. Equally true is that children born into families of means have an unmerited advantage over those living in poverty. Granted, children of means must be educated and motivated to succeed in life. However, they have been conditioned to do so at birth. In view of this, any perceived success they achieve in life is expected, and not due to special qualities they possess compared to those born into poverty. The question of fairness is immaterial. Because in the absence of intervention by an omnipotent God, the fate of most people is determined by where they were born and what they were taught.

RELIGION

The last factor to consider within cultures is religion. In the Western World, Christianity has been the dominant religion for over two thousand years. However, in places like Europe, Christianity is the religion of choice, but not one that dictates governmental policies and laws because in many ways, the social programs in European countries have reduced the influence and control of the Church. In the United States, though, Christianity remains influential and important in the lives of millions. And although greatly diminished, Christianity still influences the laws enacted by Congress.

Whether one is born in Europe or the United States, they have the freedom to believe or not to believe in the main religion of their country. And frankly, there are no negative consequences for them if they choose not to believe. That is not true for those born in Muslim or Hindu countries; moreover, there are extreme consequences for those who reject Islam or Hinduism in these countries. And these consequences can determine one's fate and perhaps life. In view of this, one's religion or that of the state can dictate their quality of life. That quality of life may have nothing to do with one's abilities or desires. Instead, it's determined by their religious culture, a culture that may suppress individual liberties to support the agenda of the state.

No one can control where they were born and to whom. Nevertheless, the factors of upbringing, culture, and living environment will affect every aspect of one's life because intellect, talent, or athletic abilities cannot always lift one from poverty if born in the wrong place. Although we applaud when someone achieves success against all odds, these individuals are the exceptions. The sad reality is that poor people born in Third World countries remain so. Even in the United States, many poor people stay poor while rich people stay rich because the factors of poverty are hard to overcome. Despite this reality, people born in the United States have avenues to overcome their upbringing. However, for them to take advantage of these avenues, they must overcome the factors against them. Sometimes though, one beats the odds because of their religious faith—a mysterious factor that is hard to calculate, but one that gives people hope against all odds.

In the book of Proverbs, there are verses that address child-rearing and the power of the rich. Although these verses are short, they are profound and apply to us today.

> Train up a child in the way he should go, And when he is old he will not depart from it. The rich rules over the poor, And the borrower is servant to the lender.
>
> —(Prov. 22:6–7)

NATURAL OCCURRENCES CATEGORY

Every year, thousands of people in the world are killed or injured by natural disasters. Many times, these natural disasters provide warning signs. For example, in the United States, some regions of the country have tornado seasons, while other regions have hurricane seasons. These weather patterns have atmospheric factors that can be measured. In view of this, it's possible to predict potential storm systems by measuring these factors. Hence, if storms can be predicted, people can be warned to seek shelter.

In view of this, taking shelter after being warned of a storm is crucial. People living in states where tornadoes or hurricanes are common understand how dangerous these storms can be. So they take these warning sirens seriously and seek shelter immediately. As a result, many lives are saved because they reacted properly. Conversely, people traveling through or visiting states during a tornado or hurricane may underestimate the dangers associated with them. Hence, they may not seek shelter immediately during a tornado or hurricane. This delay could cost them their lives or result in serious injury.

Unlike tornadoes and hurricanes, earthquakes are harder to detect. Earthquakes occur when tectonic plates (large slabs of rock underground) move, which trigger fault lines to shake. For example, in California, the fault lines are constantly stressed because of the Pacific Ocean's tectonic plate. Although the fault lines in this part of the country are constantly stressed, most residents don't overreact during minor tremors. Therefore, people living on the Pacific Coast understand that major earthquakes are possible, so they are less likely to panic when one does occur.

This is important since there is no safe shelter during an earthquake; however, knowing how to react during one is crucial. Because the key during an earthquake is not to panic and position yourself away from objects or structures that could fall on you. In places like California, people have been taught what to do during an earthquake. In addition, many buildings and homes in California have been built to withstand some ground movement during an earthquake. Therefore, residents living there have some assurance their homes won't collapse on them during a quake.

This is not true for people living in Third World countries where earthquakes are common. Because in these countries, they don't have the resources to educate their people nor fund emergency units that can respond quickly after a disaster. Thus, many people in these countries get injured or killed during an earthquake because they panic. Unfortunately, many who do survive an earthquake initially die because they don't receive medical assistance quickly.

Although predicting an earthquake is difficult, it's possible to project. In regions of the world where earthquakes are common, there are instruments that can measure seismic activity prior to a major earthquake. Although this information cannot always predict when an earthquake might occur, it can be used to alert those in authority that one is possible. In view of this, leaders in these areas can have contingency plans in place if one does occur.

Natural disasters like tornadoes, hurricanes, and earthquakes do not discriminate. The good and bad people get injured or killed during one. Many people want to blame fate or divine judgment when loved ones die in a natural disaster overseas. The truth is these individuals were just in the wrong place at the wrong time. Perhaps if they knew the risks in these areas for storms or quakes, they may have reacted differently during one. Still, even if they knew the correct steps to follow during a natural disaster, there is no guarantee they would have survived it.

There are scientific explanations for why natural disasters occur. Although there has been a lot of progress in understanding why these natural events occur, they are still unpredictable and can strike at any time. The scientific community believes that the earth is constantly changing and evolving. Thus, these natural disasters are simply a by-product of a living planet in flux. Conversely, recent changes within the earth due to global warming has scientists blaming mankind for recent natural disasters.

If we concede that the earth is getting warmer, then the causes are either human activity or natural climatic changes or both. Regardless of the causes for it, there is no evidence to support that global warming is causing earthquakes, hurricanes, or tornadoes. In view of this, do we just concede that the root cause for all natural disasters is a planet that is constantly evolving? If not, what other forces could be responsible for these natural disasters?

The scientific community and most people believe there is nothing mysterious about natural disasters. They are simply a by-product of living on planet Earth. This belief, though, conflicts with how some religions and folklore view natural disasters. For example, one of the core tenets of Christianity is that the earth has been cursed due to original sin by Adam and Eve. Some Eastern religions suggest that deities are constantly fighting for control of the universe. As a result, natural disasters are a by-product of this infighting among gods.

The strongest case cited by people of faith that God or some variation of one has used natural disasters in the past is the Great Flood. There is physical evidence throughout the world to support a massive flood that covered the Earth. This evidence can be found on sea floors and in mountains through sediment and fossilized remains. In addition, every ancient culture from the past has a story about a great flood. The only variation in their stories is why it happened and what deity was responsible for it.

Natural disasters can profoundly affect people. In view of this, many people want to believe that supernatural forces are responsible for them. If so, they can accept the loss of loved ones because of a natural disaster. This is especially true in Third World counties because people in these countries don't need concrete evidence to believe in the supernatural. Conversely, people in Western countries blame global warming or atmospheric factors for violent storms and earthquakes. They have this belief because global warming and atmospheric factors can be measured and input into models. Conversely, conceding that God or dark forces are responsible for natural disasters is disconcerting and irrational.

If we concede that God created the Earth, then why did he create storms and earthquakes? Could it be possible that natural disasters are a by-product of a cursed world? Cursed in the sense that it was changed because of Adam's disobedience. In Genesis 3:17–19, we are told of Adam's punishment: "Then to Adam He said, 'Because you have heeded the voice of your wife, and have eaten from the tree of which I commanded you, saying, "You shall not eat of it:" Cursed is the ground for your sake; In toil you shall eat of it All the days of your life. Both thorns and thistles it shall bring forth for you, And you shall eat the herb of the field. In the sweet of your face you shall eat bread Till you return to the ground, For out of it you were taken; For dust you are, And to dust you shall return."'" These verses won't comfort those who lose loved ones in natural disasters, but they can provide spiritual perspective for why they occurred.

HEALTHY BODY/MIND/AND SPIRIT

The importance of a healthy body, mind, and spirit are critical factors to weigh whenever something bad happens to a good person. Although most people are aware of negative factors associated with eating unhealthy foods, they ignore the risks of being overweight and the consequences because of it. Nevertheless, they won't change their eating habits. For example, millions of Americans suffer from physical ailments due to unhealthy eating habits. Yet they won't change their eating habits until after they experience a heart attack or something worse.

Americans are divided over many issues, but the issues of overeating and its negative consequences affect all. It does not matter whether one is black or white, rich or poor, educated or high school dropout—all struggle with controlling their weight and eating healthy. The only difference is that wealthy people can afford professional help and dietary foods to address their problem. Even good people who dedicate themselves to others and society are not immune from the negative consequences of being overweight. Hence, they succumb to the same fate as the less-desirable people in our society due to this condition.

When people we know and love die due to alcoholism, drug overdose, or respiratory diseases, we accept it as a by-product of their negative choices. Seldom do we blame God or others for their tragic deaths because it's easier for us to accept their death because of their bad choices. Conversely, it's hard for us to accept a massive heart attack or cancer diagnoses when none of the big three (alcohol, smoking, drugs) were involved. Even though the causes for heart attacks and many cancers are known, we ignore these causes as possible reasons for why loved ones died. Instead, we want to blame something or someone for their fate.

Granted, many people get diagnosed with cancer every year, and there are no known reasons for it. On a personal note, I lost my grandmother to cancer, and she lived and ate healthy throughout her life. But what I don't know is the environmental factors she was exposed to in her lifetime. Likewise, there are genetic factors for cancers that have not been identified. This would explain why certain families have a history of certain types of cancers. Though we question the fairness of cancer when loved ones or good people die from it, there are reasons why they contracted this disease. The only question is what known or unknown factors were responsible for the cancer?

MIND

Although a healthy body is essential to living well, a heathy mind is crucial. When a person cannot think right because of physical or psychological damage to their brain, bad things can happen. Some people are born with mental health issues such as bipolarity, ADD (attention deficit disorder), or schizophrenia. Although these conditions can affect every aspect of one's life, they are treatable with medication. Conversely, psychological conditions are harder to detect and treat. In many ways, psychological conditions can be just as debilitating as TBI (traumatic brain injuries). For example, many returning soldiers and marines from duty in Iraq and Afghanistan are suffering from PTSD (post-traumatic stress disorder), anxiety, or depression. The medication they are prescribed for these conditions won't cure them. Instead, it simply helps them cope with their psychological scars.

When I worked as a VA counselor, I interviewed hundreds of soldiers and marines who served in Iraq and Afghanistan. Many of these service members filed claims with the VA (Veterans Administration) for mental health conditions. Anxiety and depression were claimed, most often followed by PTSD (post-traumatic stress disorder). Although most of these service members were prescribed medication for their mental health conditions, this treatment only stabilizes them from harming themselves or others. The real work required them to seek counseling for their experiences and develop coping mechanisms to deal with their emotional pain. Unfortunately, some of those veterans who refused to address their emotional scars often resorted to self-medication by using alcohol or drugs.

When loved ones or people we know commit suicide or do bad things because of their mental health problems, we understand why. This is especially true for those who suffer from bipolarity, schizophrenia, or depression. What is harder for us to accept is when a healthy person changes because of psychological trauma. Many veterans have been changed this way. Although we may understand that combat affects people, we still expect that person to recover in time.

When they don't, we question why they can't recover and resume their old lifestyle.

Whether it's PTSD or a genetic mental health condition, often parents blame themselves when they lose a child to suicide. They may even question whether God is punishing them for past sins. This is especially true for mothers. Although family members and friends offer condolences when bad things happen to a loved one, their support cannot alleviate the loss and guilt many people experience after a suicide. Parents always reflect on what role they played after the death of a child to suicide, even if the child's suicide was due to a mental health condition.

Although it may appear emotionally cold to consider the factors responsible for one's suicide, they can be used to explain why. For example, one's personality determines their response to adversity. Positive people look for the good in every situation, whereas pessimistic individuals expect bad things to happen to them. Thus, a traumatic event for a negative person can trigger desperate measures on their part. In addition, personality and one's culture, family, and personal history are factors to weigh when one suffers from mental illness. In view of this, when bad things happen to people who suffer from mental health conditions, all the factors must be weighed. A passage in Proverbs 23:7 supports the power of our thoughts: "For as he thinks in his heart, so is he. 'Eat and drink!' he says to you, But his heart is not with you."

SPIRIT

The last component of health is one's spirit. How one views their spirit or spirituality shapes how they respond to events in the world. For example, a person with faith in God reacts very differently to adversary than a nonbeliever. Although nonbelievers lack faith in God, they may have faith in the government or other agencies. Thus, everyone has faith in someone or something that governs how they live their lives. Faith does matter. The only question is whether their faith is in God or other entities.

The world has many religions with different interpretations for God. In the Western World, Christianity is the dominant religion while Islam is the primary religion in the Middle East and Asia. Although both religions believe in one God, there are few similarities in what they believe and how they worship him. Furthermore, there are variations within Christianity and Islam. For example, Christian denominations have derived from two camps: Catholic or Protestant. The main difference between Catholic and Protestant denominations is how they view the authority of the Church. In short, Protestant churches do not believe in a priesthood hierarchy whereas Catholic-derived denominations do.

When bad things happen to religious or good people, the principles of their faith can determine how they respond. Yet even those with strong belief in a god and the afterlife may struggle with the tragic death of a loved one, although their faith may lessen the psychological loss of that loved one. Conversely, if one's faith teaches that untimely deaths are God's punishment because of hidden sins, then their faith could cause more harm than good. So how one views God and the tenets of their faith can determine how they respond to loss. These responses are measurable factors.

No model can project how religious faith strengthens a person after suffering a loss. Although religious faith is not a measurable factor, the core tenets of it can be measured. Likewise, the religious culture where one resides can influence their reaction to loss. For example, Americans were shocked and fearful after 9/11. Even though the United States eventually went to war because of 9/11, Americans' initial response was one of sorrow and reflection. As a result, church attendance throughout the country increased in the months following 9/11. Many Americans responded this way because of their Christian backgrounds. Conversely, people in the Middle East or India would respond differently if their country was attacked. The key difference is what Islam and Hinduism teaches about revenge compared to that of Christianity.

When a person starts to experience physical, mental, or spiritual decline, it can affect their overall health. For example, older people commit suicide because of their physical ailments, while healthy teenagers commit suicide because their perception of self and life is distorted. Nevertheless, a strong faith in God or self can keep one from committing suicide when their physical or mental health declines. In view of this, understanding the human factors associated with declining physical, mental, and spiritual health can help loved ones accept loss.

Religious faith can also help loved ones accept loss. One physical factor that cannot be disputed: everyone dies. So it does not matter whether one is perceived as a good or bad person because physical death is inevitable. Granted, many people do things to their bodies that accelerate the aging process. Some of these things are not viewed as bad activities such as eating too much. Nevertheless, it can cut one's life short. Another example would be a cold miner that acquires black lung disease. This was not a deliberate act by him to shorten his life. Instead, it was simply a by-product of working in a dangerous field to earn a living. In view of this, blaming God, fate, or bad luck for the miner's death due to respiratory problems is denying the reason for it: an environmental factor.

The most popular public speakers in the world today are those who convey a positive message. Although most of us tend to think negatively when bad things happen to us, we admire and want to emulate those who can see the positive in any situation. Psychologically and spiritually, there is something powerful when we view things positively. This positive overview is expressed in the Bible too. We find a passage to support this in Philippians 4:8:

> Finally, brethren, whatever things are true, whatever things are noble, whatever things are just, whatever things are pure, whatever things are lovely, whatever things are of good report, if there is any virtue and if there is anything praiseworthy—meditate on these things.

THREE LAWS

Often when bad things happen to good people, we assume they are innocent of any wrongdoing because they are good people. So their plight, fate, or medical diagnosis is unjust. Therefore, we choose to ignore possible reasons that caused their misfortune. Furthermore, the possible reasons for their misfortune are endless.

What is not endless are the laws that govern them. Every misfortune can be classified into one of three laws: the law of man, nature, or God.

Under the law of man, what is legal or illegal can vary greatly from state to state, whereas violating foreign laws can end your life. A good example of this are drug offenses overseas. How often do we hear stories of Americans going overseas and getting caught with drugs? Seldom do these individuals escape prison, and their living conditions are horrendous. Conversely, this same drug offense in the United States would be plea bargained to probation or a fine.

In view of this, if a loved one or friend breaks some law in a foreign country—whether it's just or unjust—are they at fault? If based on American principles and laws, that person did nothing wrong. For example, criticizing human rights or freedom of speech in an Islamic country could be considered treason. Hence, if one loses their freedom or life because of this action, do we blame that country for an unjust law? Furthermore, do we have the right to judge whether a foreign law is just?

This sense of injustice occurs in the United States too because laws are not enforced evenly across the country, and the justice system is not color-blind. Furthermore, states have different punishments for the same crime. For example, if you get charged for murder in Texas, a death sentence is probable. Yet in California, the worst sentence you receive for murder is life in prison. And the recent legalization of marijuana in some states has changed the landscape for drug-related charges. Nevertheless, some states still arrest and charge people for possession of marijuana. In short, where you live and what you do can have profound consequences if you break the law. The fairness of those consequences is immaterial because you broke the law of the land. Your argument that "I am a good person" cannot be used to escape punishment for breaking the law.

LAWS OF NATURE

Although what constitutes breaking man-made laws can vary from country to country, breaking natural laws have no variations. An American or Italian will experience the same fate if they break a law of nature. In addition, breaking laws of nature can occur naturally or the result of human activity. For example, toxins that are released into the air or water can cause sickness and death. And many times, the victims of environmental factors have no idea they were exposed or vulnerable to a hazard. The recent incident of water contamination in Flint, Michigan, was a perfect example because the residents of Flint did not know about the contaminated water until after it caused permanent damage to those exposed.

In addition, environmental hazards such as Agent Orange, asbestos, and lead paint exposure have caused great harm to thousands. Unfortunately, many of the individuals exposed to these hazards had no idea of the dangers until years later. Although we understand the risks of these hazards today, that cannot change what these individuals suffered because of these hazards. Sadly, many of these victims died due to their exposure.

In view of this, many of the victims of environmental hazards have done nothing wrong to warrant their fate. So it's not a question of fairness, but one of cause and effect. Because environmental factors don't discriminate. They affect all people equally. Furthermore, once an individual has been exposed to an environmental factor, there are uncontrolled consequences because of it. Conversely, when individuals knowingly do activities that are harmful to their bodies and minds, they are responsible for the consequences. Activities such as smoking, drug use, or alcoholism are self-inflicted wounds. Unfortunately, rarely do individuals who use these substances escape the negative effects from them.

Many people understand that there is a cause-and-effect principle when loved ones are exposed to bad things like asbestos or lead paint. Likewise, when people we know die from issues associated with alcohol, drug, or tobacco use, few question the fairness of their fate. Hence, we concede they died because of a bad habit or addiction. Once again, most people don't blame others or God for their demise. However, being informed that a family member or friend has cancer or suffered a massive heart attack is viewed differently as we don't associate these medical conditions with personal responsibility.

When I was a teenager, a young family moved into our neighborhood. They had two young children. In appearance and reality, they were a model family. The father and mother loved each other, and they were great parents. No one in the family had any issues with drugs, alcohol, or smoking. The only warning sign in their household that something bad could happen in the future was their eating habits. In short, they enjoyed eating; however, they ate to excess.

They eventually moved away to Arizona. Years later, my parents moved to Arizona as well. Once there, they resumed their friendship. While visiting my parents years later, I saw this family again. They were still this great family that anyone would love to have as neighbors. Unfortunately, both the father and son had gained a lot of weight. I mentioned to my parents that perhaps they should express some concern about their weight gain. But for obvious reasons, they did not feel it was their place.

Shortly after my visit, the father died of a massive heart attack. He was in his midfifties when he died. I was shocked to hear the news, and I could not find any words to comfort his wife. I thought often about this man and how he died. He was extremely intelligent, a strong Catholic by all accounts, a great worker, father, and husband. In short, his death was the type of personal loss that makes one contemplate, Why did this bad thing happen to this good person? No doubt his widow wrestled with this question too.

This man only had one negative factor that caused his premature death. He ate to excess, which caused him to gain a lot of weight. This factor violated the law of nature. As a result, he had a heart attack because of his body fat. Though it seemed unfair that a gifted man died so young, no one can be blamed for his demise except for him. Unfortunately, this type of scenario occurs every day in our world. Though we want to blame someone or God for the tragic death of a loved one, perhaps the individual who died was responsible for his fate.

LAWS OF GOD

The third law to consider when bad things happen to good people is the law of God. If God does exist, then he has rules for humanity to follow. However, your view of God can either uplift or depress you when bad things happen. For example, if you view God as a taskmaster who demands perfection, your entire life will revolve around fear—fear that you are not good enough, fear that you're doing the wrong things, fear that God is ready to punish you. This God-fear belief is taught to you based on your culture and upbringing.

It's impossible to explain all the attributes of God or deities that people in the world believe in. For example, in India, they believe in over 300 million gods. Even within Christianity, there are over forty thousand denominations in the world, and their interpretation of the Bible can vary greatly. Given all the religions in the world that believe in God or some variation of one, can anyone prove that he exists? If so, how does God exercise control or punishment over people? Likewise, can man devise a model based on factors that can prove the workings of God in the world?

The existence of God is hard to prove. Yet I do believe a God model is possible by eliminating probable factors and conceding to supernatural ones. In view of this, we must concede that based on religious faith throughout the world that a God or energy source created the universe. If so, how does this God entity operate? How does he watch what humans do? Intervene in the affairs of mankind? In short, what are his or its parameters for intervention in the affairs of humanity? And if there are parameters to follow, what is the source for them?

Clearly models can predict results if the right factors are plugged in. Therefore, understanding if God is punishing one should be possible if the right factors are known. Since everything in the universe is governed by laws, there must be some entity or force that established those laws. If we identify the author of the universe, he or it created a code for us to obey. If this spiritual code of conduct exists, we must find it and live by it. So yes, I believe that a model with known factors can predict bad things for people that violate God's laws.

There are several verses in the Bible that cite the importance of obeying the laws of man and God. A good summation of these verses can be found in the book of Romans. In Romans 13:1–3, we're told about authority and its purpose: "Let every soul be subject to the governing authorities. For there is no authority except from God, and the authorities that exist are appointed by God. Therefore whoever resists the authority resists the ordinance of God, and those who resist will bring judgment on themselves. For rulers are not a terror to good works, but to evil. Do you want to be unafraid of the authority? Do what is good, and you will have praise from the same."

SATAN/KARMA

The belief in karma permeates every culture in the world. Even in regions of the world where religious faith is not strong, people believe in karma. In Buddhism and Hinduism, karma refers to one's state and destiny based on how they live. Hence, if they act or live poorly in their current life or state, they cannot reach the next stage of existence. However, people in the Western World have decided that karma means you get what you deserve. Thus, when someone we dislike suffers misfortune, we're quick to invoke bad karma on that individual, even though their misfortune may have had nothing to do with anything they did or said. Nevertheless, many of us applaud when bad things happen to bad people, especially if that person has wronged us.

This belief in karma is shared by religious people too, even though most religions believe in a literal devil or evil force in the world. Thus, it's the devil or evil force that is responsible for mankind's troubles. Despite this religious tenet, many believers have more faith in karma than a literal devil. The main reason for this belief is our culture. Our culture conveys messages via television, internet, and the radio that stressing secular principles concerning karma. For example, adages like "What goes around comes around," "You get what you deserve," and "People in glass houses should not throw stones" are common phrases that people truly believe in. As a result, when misfortune happens to a perceived villain in our society, karma gets the credit for invoking justice on that individual.

This leads us to a question: are there factors that can be plugged into a model that can predict karma? Moreover, can we prove that karma is a supernatural law that is triggered by certain acts of individuals? The short answer is that karma is a belief principle. And like many beliefs in the world today, those who believe need no proof. Yet for those who do not believe, no proof will persuade otherwise. Granted, there is something at work that is causing bad things to happen to bad people. No doubt there are known factors that are causing bad things to happen to people. In view of this, when known factors cannot be identified, do we concede that karma is responsible?

SATAN

Although belief in karma is subjective, a belief in Satan is not. For Christians, Satan is the adversary. His job is to dissuade people from trusting in Jesus Christ for their salvation. If he cannot prevent their salvation, his job is to discourage the faithful through trials and tribulations. Although most Christians view Satan in this way, there are strong disagreements within churches to the extent of his power and whether he is real.

Some Christian denominations view Satan as a formidable adversary that rules the entire world with an iron fist. Others see him as the enemy, but he lacks any authority or power to cause bad things to happen to good people. Thus, he can only torment non-believers, but not Christians. A third view of Satan is that he is not real, but a fabrication by the Early Church to scare people into salvation. Hence, Christians during the Dark Ages became loyal followers of the Church and conceded all authority to it. Likewise, some liberal churches today also contend that Satan never existed. He was just created to ease our guilty subconscious when we do something wrong. Hence, the phrase "The devil made me do it" was born.

Hollywood seldom portrays Satan as an evil presence that plagues mankind. Instead, he is portrayed as an individual that is misunderstood. They suggest that Satan is simply an angel that fell out of grace with God. As a result, any bad things he does is to get people to change their ways. Conversely, Hollywood contends that Christians have mischaracterized Satan's persona. They imply that pastors do this to scare believers into coming to church.

Often, Satan's image on television is benign; however, Hollywood reverses the script with movies. Satan's image in movies is that of an evil force that possesses people, which causes them to do bad things. Hollywood portrays Satan both ways for financial reasons because there is money to be made by portraying Satan as an innocent fallen angel and that of an evil being. In short, the entertainment industry is simply capitalizing on people's real or perceived image of the devil.

So the question is what role does Satan play when bad things happen to good people? The first Satan factor to ponder is whether he is real or not. If so, what evidence is there to prove he exists? Unfortunately, any evidence concerning a literal devil would be subjective in nature, not tangible. Because if Satan is a spiritual being, he is invisible. Nevertheless, his evil acts are tangible things that can be measured. Thus, demonic activity can be felt, seen, and heard by its victims and others.

In view of this, demonic activity can be verified by eliminating all tangible factors that could apply. So if we eliminate probable causes for an event, it may be due to improbable causes. Thus, the paranormal factor is something that can be measured. If it can be measured, then it's possible that one's misfortune occurred because of an evil force.

There are many verses in the Bible that mention Satan. Although the Bible is clear concerning the authority that Satan has in the world today, many people still wonder why there is evil in the world. In the book of Matthew, we get an answer about the devil and his authority.

> Again, the devil took Him up on an exceedingly high mountain, and showed Him all the kingdoms of the world and their glory. And he said to Him, "All these things I will give You if You will fall down and worship me." Then Jesus said to him, "Away with you, Satan! For it is written, You shall worship the Lord your God, and Him only you shall serve."
>
> —(Matt. 4:8–10)

GOD/RELIGION

Throughout recorded history, mankind has believed in God or some variation of one. The question is why? There are many reasons people give for believing in God. The main reason is that people want to believe that someone is overseeing the universe. If so, then someday, he or it will intervene and fix the world. Likewise, there is a belief in eternal life for those who live good and worship God. So this motivates people to pray and to hope their prayers will be answered.

There are many religions that believe in God or deities, but only three that truly believe in one God: Christianity, Islam, and Judaism. Ironically, these three religions have fought holy wars over whose God is real. Christian kings, for example, conducted the Crusades from the eleventh through fifteenth centuries. Sometimes their foes were Jews, and other times they were Muslims. In the end though, many of these military campaigns failed. Yet they created animosity and mistrust for future generations. As a result, extremist groups like ISIS use past Muslim atrocities to motivate converts against the West and Israel. However, Israel's distrust of European initiatives and motives are based on past atrocities too. For example, the killing of six million Jews by Germany during World War II still dictates how Israel responds to outside threats.

So often God gets the blame for the acts people do in the name of religion. A recent example of this are the attacks of 9/11. Islamic extremists were responsible for the attacks of 9/11. Yet Muslims were blamed for it. Conversely, some conservative churches cited these attacks as God's moral judgment against the United States for its immorality. Even though none of these religious views can prove it was God's will, he gets the credit and blame for the attacks of 9/11. In fact, God probably had nothing to do with these attacks or the reasons for them. Nevertheless, many people want to link this disaster with supernatural judgment.

If God does exist, are there limitations to what he can or will do? Moreover, does God operate based on the tenets of a specific religion? If so, which one? These questions must be answered to determine if God plays a role in why bad things happen to good people. Furthermore, agreeing on the factors that prove God's intent or involvement in an event could be difficult. But it's necessary to prove the theory that all bad events can be calculated by using factors within models. Still, devising a God model will be difficult to create, but one that could be more valuable than all the other models combined.

If a God model could be devised, what would be the basis for its factors? In Islam and Christianity, there are holy books that outline the tenets of the faith. In view of this, are the verses in the Koran and Bible instructions from God? If so, why has mankind resisted the laws, principles, and statutes of these religious books? There can only be two reasons for this resistance: the Koran and Bible are either not divinely inspired, or there is something about our nature that refuses to obey.

If God created the universe, then he must have left some instructions for mankind to follow. The dominant religion in the Western World is Christianity. In Christianity, the Bible is considered God's Word. If we concede that the Bible is God's Word, are there instructions in it for us to follow? Although most Christians believe that God inspired the Bible, there are sharp differences in how Christian denominations interpret Scripture. So getting consensus among Christians will require some work. This is especially true for how Catholics and Protestants interpret Scripture. Thus, if these differences can be reconciled, then perhaps the answers for why bad things happen to good people can be found within the pages of the Bible.

Chapter 2

SATAN/KARMA

Few would dispute there is evil in the world. The only disagreement is why there is evil in the world. Sociologists contend people are simply a by-product of their culture. So if they do evil acts that are acceptable within their culture, they are not evil. Conversely, they contend different cultures have no right to judge other ones that practice different values and religious beliefs. In short, no one is right nor wrong, but a by-product of their culture.

The argument against this premise is that many people reject their cultural values and beliefs. If people reject their cultural norms, then what governs their behavior? If it's based on free will, then why do some people behave responsibly while others are irresponsible? If individuality or free will determines how one acts within a culture, then why would a person choose to reject acceptable behavior when there are negative consequences for doing so? This seems to conflict with the theory that we evolved because of our superior intelligence. Granted, our technology has evolved, but mankind's behavior has not.

Sociologists have conducted many research studies concerning the moral beliefs of primitive cultures. These studies often show that primitive cultures share common moral beliefs as those in Western countries. For example, the acts of stealing, murder, coveting, false witness, adultery, or disrespect for parents were always considered wrong things to do within cultures. Even within cultures where traditional religious beliefs are not taught, people have a sense of what is right and wrong. This moral paradigm can be observed among children with no religious upbringing too. So clearly, human beings have been imprinted with something at birth that provides them with a moral compass. Therefore, if we are born with a moral compass or soul, do we concede God is responsible for it?

If mankind was created with a moral compass or soul, then why do so many people reject the religious tenets of their culture? For example, 70 percent of Americans consider themselves Christians, but many of them do not attend church often, nor do they practice the moral teachings of the faith. In view of this, are these individuals Christians? If not, what are the factors that prove one is a Christian?

Most theologians would agree that Christians believe Jesus Christ was the Son of God who died for their sins. Likewise, because of Jesus, mankind's relationship with God the Father was restored, a relationship that was severed because of Adam's original sin in the garden. Although there are many Christian denominations in the world, the belief that Jesus was the Son of God unites all believers.

Satan

Two other principles of Christianity most theologians agree on are that our soul never dies, and we have free will. The Bible seems to imply that angels and demons are immortal too, and they have free will. This is important because it provides an explanation for evil in the world because evil is not a feeling, but a negative force that is afflicting mankind. The Bible is clear there is evil in the world because of Satan and his demons. Satan is called the adversary because he torments mankind and prevents Christians from doing good works. If true, then why did God create a devil?

In the book of Revelation, we are told about Satan's punishment for defying God:

> And war broke out in heaven: Michael and his angels fought with the dragon; and the dragon and his angels fought, but they did not prevail, nor was a place found for them

> in heaven and longer. So the great dragon was cast out, that serpent of old, called the Devil and Satan, who deceives the whole world; he was cast to the earth, and his angels were cast out with him.
>
> —(Rev. 12:7-9)

These verses clearly outline the devil's fate and the consequences for mankind because of it.

God did not create a devil; he created an archangel name Lucifer. His fall from heaven was due to his disobedience. Satan's coup in heaven occurred because he believed his power rivaled that of God's—even though God created him. And clearly, he had unique powers and gifts other angels believed in. This was evident because one-third of the angels in heaven followed him. I think many theologians have underestimated how powerful and gifted Satan was in heaven.

Satan still has power today, which he uses to attack mankind and cause bad things to happen in the world. His main weapons are demonic persuasion and temptation. Satan uses these weapons to attack our minds with negative thoughts. Despite this, people have free will to reject or accept his evil thoughts. Therefore, for a demonic thought to take hold, a person must agree with it and then act on it. Even original sin by Adan and Eve was an agreement to do what Satan suggested.

Sadly, one of the consequences for mankind because of original sin was forfeiting control of the earth to Satan. We find many verses in the New Testament to support this claim. For example, in the book of Matthew, there is an interplay between Jesus and the devil. We find this in Matthew 4:8–10:

> Again, the devil took Him up on an exceedingly high mountain, and showed Him all the kingdoms of the world and their glory. And he said to Him, "All these

> things I will give You if You will fall down and worship me." Then Jesus said to him, "Away with you, Satan! For it is written, You shall worship the Lord your God, and Him only you shall serve."

Clearly these verses state Satan has authority to influence the affairs of mankind. Furthermore, it provides us insight for understanding why there is evil in the world.

The verses in Matthew 4:8–10 are an overview of Satan's authority in the world. We find in the book of Job evidence that Satan has permission to attack and torment those who do not belong to God. In Job 1:6–8, we are informed of Satan's activities:

> Now there was a day when the sons of God came to present themselves before the Lord, and Satan also came among them. And the Lord said to Satan, "From where do you come?" So Satan answered the Lord and said, "From going to and fro on the earth, and from walking back and forth on it." Then the Lord said to Satan, "Have you considered My servant Job, that there is none like him on the earth, a blameless and upright man, one who fears God and shuns evil?"

These verses confirm that Satan is looking for opportunities to attack someone. We know this because God mentions Job to Satan. God mentions Job because he is a man of great faith. Satan, therefore, needed permission and a reason to attack Job. We get confirmation of this in Job 1:9–12:

> So Satan answered the Lord and said, "Does Job fear God for nothing? "Have

> You not made a hedge around him, around his household, and around all that he has on every side? You have blessed the work of his hands, and his possessions have increased in the land. "But now, stretch out Your hand and touch all that he has, and he will surely curse You to your face!" And the Lord said to Satan, "Behold, all that he has is in your power; only do not lay a hand on his person." So Satan went out from the presence of the Lord.

The message of these verses is clear: Satan needs permission to attack a person of faith. Likewise, it's clear that Satan has the authority to attack and inflict harm on people. Conversely, these verses confirm God's hedge of protection surrounding believers. Unfortunately for Job, he had to endure the full wrath of Satan because God allowed it. And in the process, Job loses all his possessions, children, health, and reputation among family and friends. Even though Job was afflicted unjustly, God allowed it to prove a point to Satan. In view of this, clearly Job had a case to question why bad things happen to a good person. Despite this, at the end of the story, God restores all of Job's wealth and reputation. Nevertheless, he is never told the reason for his suffering.

Many Christians believe Satan was defeated when Jesus Christ died on the cross for our sins. Hence, his authority to attack and torment Christians ended two thousand years ago. The Bible seems to support this position. Still, a Christian must live a life that honors God if they want his hedge of protection from the attacks of Satan and his demons. We find in 1 Peter 5:8–9 confirmation of this: "Be sober, be vigilant; because your adversity the devil walks about like a roaring lion, seeking whom he may devour." Peter is not talking to nonbelievers. He is talking to Christians. Therefore, Christians must keep their focus on Jesus Christ by living a life that honors God. If not, there are negative spiritual consequences.

Even people of faith struggle with thinking patterns that are considered sinful. Feelings of anger, hate, bitterness, lust, envy, pride, unforgiveness, and covetousness can diminish or destroy a Christian's testimony for Christ. Once a Christian loses their testimony for Christ because of bad behavior or thinking patterns, they open the door to attacks from Satan. Furthermore, God is not obligated to keep his hedge of protection around Christians who won't forgive others and confess their sins. This is outlined in John 10:10: "The thief does not come except to steal, and to kill, and to destroy. I have come that they may have life, and that they may have it more abundantly."

FULL ARMOR

Given this powerful warning concerning Satan, how can anyone fight off these dark thoughts and avoid bad behaviors that will destroy their testimony for Christ? The Bible provides us answers in Ephesians 6:10–18:

> Finally, my brethren, be strong in the Lord and in the power of His might. Put on the whole armor of God, that you may be able to stand against the wiles of the devil. For we do not wrestle against flesh and blood, but against principalities, against powers, against rulers of the darkness of this age, against spiritual hosts of wickedness in the heavenly places. Therefore take up the whole armor of God, that you may be able to withstand in the evil day, and having done all, to stand. Stand therefore, having girded your waist with truth, having put on the breast plate of righteousness, and having shod your feet with the preparation

> of the gospel of peace; above all, taking the shield of faith with which you will be able to quench all the fiery darts of the wicked one. And take the helmet of salvation, and the sword of the Spirit, which is the word of God; praying always with all prayer and supplication in the Spirit, being watchful to this end with all perseverance and supplication for all saints—

These verses outline all the evil forces against Christians and the means to confront them. However, one must discern the symbolic language used in these verses. For example, putting on the whole armor of God is a metaphor for the three spiritual weapons Christians need to confront Satan and his demons: the helmet, shield, and sword. The helmet is symbolic for controlling your thoughts. Satan's greatest weapon is deception through our thoughts. Thus, bad thinking will produce bad results. Our main protection against the attacks of Satan is God. This is what the shield represents. To fight the enemy, we use the sword. The sword is symbolic for the Word of God. In short, you cite Scripture when dark thoughts or situations arise.

The whole armor of God is not difficult to understand; however, applying it to your life is difficult. It's difficult because you must fight your flesh—your human nature, the world, and Satan. The battle to defeat these three impediments is not a physical one, but a battle of your mind. You must determine in your mind that God is the source for your strength, and through faith in him, you can overcome any obstacle. Because we are what we think; we think what we are. In short, you must have fanatical faith in God to fight off the attacks of Satan and his demons. This can only be achieved by knowing God—not by knowing about him. You know God by praying and meditating, reading your Bible consistently, and learning to listen to the inner voice of the Holy Spirit.

The next component of the whole armor of God is the helmet. The helmet is a symbolic reference for controlling what you see and think. Hence, what you watch on television, the music you listen to, and people you interact with all affect how you think. And if all these activities along with the people you associate with belittle or ignore the things of God, you'll be vulnerable to attacks from the enemy. That is the message of Ephesians 6:10–18.

To get your mind to think correctly and holy, you must put information into it that points toward God. No, you don't abandon all your friends and family, but you need to change what you watch on television, listen to on the radio, and the people you want to be around. In addition, you must be involved with a church and read your Bible often. These changes are just the first steps. The hard part is allowing the Holy Spirit to take more control of your life. This cannot occur until you are willing to change how you think, act, and believe.

The last component of the whole armor of God is the sword. The sword briefly is knowing Scripture or your Bible. In practical terms, it's knowing what the Bible says about a given situation. For example, you're feeling tired and defeated concerning a situation or person. A verse for this situation would be "I can do all things through Christ who strengthens me." By citing God's Word, instead of resorting to the things of the world, you are expressing faith in God. Remember, God is only obligated to intervene for a person when they express faith in him. However, it takes time and experience to develop faith in Scripture when things go wrong. Hence, the same mentality that one needs to prepare for a marathon applies to faith in Scripture too. In short, you must apply biblical principles into your daily routine.

Even after a Christian learns how to fully apply the whole armor of God, they are not exempt from demonic attacks. We find confirmation of this in 2 Corinthians 12:7: "And lest I should be exalted above measure by the abundance of the revelations, a thorn in the flesh was given to me, a messenger of Satan to buffet me, lest I be exalted above measure." This is Paul talking to the Corinthians about his suffering for the cause of Christ. Although Paul did nothing worthy of torment by this demon, God allowed it to keep him humbled. Even though Paul was perhaps the greatest Christian who ever lived, he still had to keep his natural man—sin nature in check by relying on God. Hence, this tormenting spirit kept Paul grounded and focused on Jesus Christ.

The main point of 2 Corinthians 12:7 is that God allowed Paul to be tormented by this demon. We don't know how Paul was tormented, but clearly it bothered him. This is confirmed in 2 Corinthians 12:8–9: "Concerning this thing I pleaded with the Lord three times that it might depart from me. And He said to me, 'My grace is sufficient for you, for My strength is made perfect in weakness.'"

Even though no man suffered more than Paul for the cause of Christ, God still refused to cast off this tormenting spirit. Paul knew why: "Lest I be exalted above measure." Paul understood that sometimes suffering is necessary to keep us grounded. Many Christians today refuse to believe God sometimes allows suffering for his purposes.

CHURCH VIEWS

The Church today has three views concerning Satan. The first view is that Satan was defeated two thousand years ago. So Christians have nothing to fear from Satan and his demons because he was defeated when Christ died on the cross. The second view is that Satan is a roaring lion ready to pounce on you. Thus, any sinful activity can instantly cause a demonic attack. The last view contends that Satan never existed. Instead, he was created during the Dark Ages to keep people fearful and loyal to the Church. Many nonbelievers share this view today. Sadly, many Christians doubt the existence of a literal devil too.

If the devil is not real, then why did Jesus Christ die on the cross for our sins? The answer was to restore our relationship with God because of original sin by Adam and Eve. Satan caused mankind's separation from God when he deceived Eve into eating the forbidden fruit in the garden. In view of this, one cannot claim to be a Christian and doubt the existence of Satan. Because since the fall, mankind has been thrown into a spiritual war between good versus evil. This is a war for the souls of mankind. Unfortunately, many Christians do not understand this war. As a result, Satan and his demons are ruling the earth with an iron fist. Hence, the spiritual condition of the world won't change until Christians exercise their authority over Satan in Jesus's name.

If mankind is locked in this spiritual war between the forces of good versus evil, then why aren't pastors preaching on this subject to their congregations? There are three possible reasons. First, pastors are scared to lose their ministries because this message is not popular or uplifting. Second, many churches today have lukewarm Christians who lack faith in Christ and the authority of Scripture, so they cannot accept or discern deep spiritual issues. The third possible reason is outlined in 2 Corinthians 11:13–15. These verses warn about false teachers:

> For such are false apostles, deceitful workers, transforming themselves into apostles of Christ. And no wonder! For Satan himself transforms himself into an angel of light. Therefore it is no great thing if his ministers also transform themselves into ministers of righteousness, whose end will be according to their works.

Most Christian churches today are pastored by men and women who believe Jesus Christ is the Son of God. So I don't believe the warning in 2 Corinthians 11:13–15 applies to most pastors today. However, clearly there are Christian ministers who are deceiving their congregations. Sadly, the main culprit for the decline of Christianity in the United States is our culture. Likewise, because Christians won't reject the secular messages of our culture, this has weakened the Church. In view of this, Satan has the Church in disarray while he is causing havoc throughout the world.

FACTORS

There are many factors that are responsible for why bad things happen to good people. The main reason is Satan and his demons. Yes, Satan is a very powerful factor that can be blamed for many of the bad things in the world. However, there are different aspects or factors associated with Satan. The first Satan factor is God does not protect nonbelievers. Our opinion of who is considered good does not matter to God. Because if one is not born again, they are not justified before God. In Matthew 19:17, Jesus confirms this: "So He said to him, 'Why do you call Me good? No one is good but One, that is, God. But if you want to enter into life, keep the commandments.'"

Another Satan factor pertains to Christians who openly sin and don't forgive. Although a Christian's spirit is born again, their soul is not. The soul is our thoughts, emotions, and will. Thus, all Christians must be vigilant to keep their soul and spirit lined up. This cannot be done through human efforts. Instead, it must be done by submitting to the urges of the Holy Spirit that resides in every Christian's heart. When Christians ignore or refuses to listen to the Holy Spirit, they start a process of disengagement with God. Furthermore, when they engage in sinful activities that destroy their testimony for Christ, they subsequently trigger spiritual consequences. Although a single sinful act may not trigger these spiritual consequences, a refusal to repent of it will.

There are many stories in the Bible about men of faith who fell out of fellowship with God because of sin. Many of these men repented and turned back to God; however, some never repented and died because of their disobedience. Christians too can engage in sinful activities that will break their fellowship with God. As a result, they open themselves up to demonic attacks. For example, excessive drinking or drug use will destroy a Christian's testimony for Christ; moreover, they could lose their life because of it. Likewise, hidden sins such as pornography, gambling, unforgiveness, and bitterness will demoralize Christians, and they will lose their faith in God too. These hidden sins can also generate feelings of hopelessness and doubts of one's salvation. Unfortunately, some Christians even succumb to suicide because of their despair.

When Christians fall out of fellowship with God, they are vulnerable to attacks from Satan. Although Satan cannot read your mind, he can discern patterns of behavior that provides him an opportunity to attack you. We get warnings of this in 1 Peter 5:8 and in the book of Job. No, Satan is not everywhere, but he has many demons. These demons have areas of responsibility and individuals to watch over. Although a Christian's spirit is born again, their soul is not. Our soul constantly wars against the inner voice of the Holy Spirit. So if an unconfessed sin becomes ingrained in a Christian's soul, Satan has control. Once Satan has control, bad things can happen. Although God is love, he cannot allow Christians to sin with impunity. In view of this, God's hedge of protection from Satan can be lifted from Christians that fail to repent of known sins.

Many Christians and nonbelievers know negative results can occur when people do bad things. Yet often they want to blame someone for it. As a result, when loved ones or friends suffer because of bad choices, Christians may cite Satan as the culprit, while nonbelievers may claim karma as the reason for their fate. Conversely, it's hard for Christians to accept that people who live for the Lord suffer in life. For instance, the tragic loss of a child or spouse without warning can shake even the strongest person of faith. Likewise, a terminal medical diagnosis of self can invoke fear and anger that God cannot be trusted.

Although Christians know that Satan is responsible for many of the bad things that happen in the world directly or indirectly—indirectly due to original sin—it's still hard to accept. In addition, it's hard for believers to understand why God allows Satan to attack his children for no apparent reason. Although it's frustrating, like Job of the Old Testament, sometimes Christians suffer for unknown reasons.

KARMA

Another Satan factor is karma. Ironically, many Christians have more belief in Karma than a literal devil. What is karma? I believe Ephesians 6:12 gives us the answer: "For we do not wrestle against flesh and blood, but against principalities, against powers, against rulers of the darkness of this age, against spiritual hosts of wickedness in the heavenly places." Clearly this Scripture is outlining dark forces that are formidable and hard to defeat. Paul does not explain how these evil forces attack or hinder us. What he does tell us is to put on the whole armor of God.

I believe karma is a code word for demonic forces controlled by Satan. Hence, the words *principalities*, *powers*, *rulers of this age*, and *spiritual hosts of wickedness* in Ephesians 6:12 are referring to an evil force controlled by Satan. Each level of this evil force has specific areas of responsibility. This force is an army of demons with authority to harm the body, mind, and spirit. Within this evil force, there are ranks and powers assigned to demons. The strongest demons are those that rule over nations. These demonic spirits affect all nations. They are assigned to countries based on past sins of the land. For example, I believe the past sin of the United States is slavery. Thus, a spirit of racial prejudice permeates our country today.

We can find evidence of this in the book of Deuteronomy. God tells Jacob the awards for his nation if they're obedient. Conversely, Jacob is told the negative consequences if they are disobedient. The blessings are listed in Deuteronomy 28:1–3:

> Now it shall come to pass, if you diligently obey the voice of the Lord your God, to observe carefully all His commandments which I command you today, that the Lord your God will set you high above all nations of the earth. And all these blessings shall come upon you and overtake you, because you obey the voice of the Lord your God: Blessed shall you be in the city, and blessed shall you be in the country.

Conversely, God's warning for a nation that is disobedience is listed in Deuteronomy 28:15–16:

> But it shall come to pass, if you do not obey the voice of the Lord your God, to observe carefully all His commandments and His statutes which I command you today, that all these curses will come upon you and overtake you: Cursed shall you be in the city, and cursed shall you be in the country.

These verses were not just for the nation of Israel, but for all countries. I believe that God has put in place spiritual consequences for nations that reject him and his commandments. One factor of these spiritual consequences is demonic oppression for a nation that rejects him and subsequently crosses a spiritual line. For example, the United States has always been considered a Christian country, but those core biblical principles are now under attack. Even Christians have compromised their beliefs because of the culture. The result is that our country is divided, and no one knows how to unite it. This extends to the Church too because one fraction of the Church insists biblical principles cannot be compromised to appease the culture, while other fractions believe Christians must change with the times. Yet the Bible says God does not change nor does his ways change.

TONGUE

Another aspect of karma is the power of our tongue or words to cause harm. A common adage I was told as a child was "Sticks and stones can break my bones, but words can never hurt me." It is perhaps the greatest lie children are told. Harsh words do affect children and adults. For example, most marriages end because of communication problems. These communication problems developed over time due to heated arguments, which destroyed trust and created resentment within the marriage. Many marital arguments occur because of misspoken words. Even when there are real issues within a marriage that can be resolved, how the parties speak to each other can make the difference. Unfortunately, men do not understand how their words affect women, whereas women do not understand men yell without thinking about the consequences of their words.

Most people would agree that it's difficult not to gossip, express their opinions, or respond when someone is criticizing them. Although we know there are consequences for speaking our mind, we still do it. In the book of James, we are told about the tongue. We find this in James 3:8: "But no man can tame the tongue. It is an unruly evil, full of deadly poison". If this was the only verse in the Bible that spoke about the tongue, we could consider it as a metaphor. However, there are many biblical verses concerning the tongue and how it affects us. In James 3:5–6, we get a detailed description of the wrongs of the tongue:

> Even so the tongue is a little member and boasts great things. See how great a forest a little fire kindles! And the tongue is a fire, a world of iniquity. The tongue is so set among our members that it defiles the whole body, and sets on fire the course of nature; and it is set fire by hell.

The power of words to motivate or discourage is clear. Great coaches and politicians have learned that words can motivate people to do things. Conversely, harsh words can demoralize individuals—especially children. I believe God's original intent was for mankind to use his tongue for good things; however, the fall changed that purpose. In view of this, Satan knows the power we have in our tongues. So if he can get us to speak the wrong things, we set in motion negative consequence for self and others. Although many cite karma when bad things happen to people that wronged them, our ill words and feelings toward them play a role in their fate. If life and death is in the power of the tongue, then we must take responsibility for our words.

KARMA KEYS

Karma does exist. However, it's not some mysterious force that affects only people who do wrong. Instead, karma is a combination of demonic factors that are triggered by acts of individuals or nations. Many of these spiritual factors are passed on from one generation to another. Likewise, the sins of nations or regions are affixed and cannot be removed until God's people intercede on behalf of the land. Likewise, families with generational curses such as alcoholism, drug use, pornography, or suicide will continue to occur until someone breaks the curse. Family generational curses or judgments can only be broken by spirit-filled Christians.

The key factor for karma is the words we speak. The Bible is clear that our words have power to do good or evil. In Proverbs 15:1–4, we are told about the power of the tongue to do good or evil:

> A soft answer turns away wrath, But a harsh word stirs up anger. The tongue of the wise uses knowledge rightly, But the mouth of fools pours forth foolishness. The eyes of the Lord are in every place, Keeping watch on the evil and the good. A wholesome tongue is a tree of life, But perverseness in it breaks the spirit.

These verses confirm that how we use are words can affect people either positively or negatively. In Proverbs 18:21, we get a dire warning of what an evil tongue can do: "Death and life are in the power of the tongue, And those who love it will eat its fruit."

Karma has many factors that can trigger spiritual consequences for self and others. Yet Satan is the architect of all evil. Unfortunately, many pastors won't preach sermons about Satan and his demons. They avoid this subject because the message is not positive, and their congregations are spiritually immature. Although pastors boldly proclaim the defeat of Satan when Jesus Christ died on then cross, they won't preach about generational curses and judgments because these issues require a greater understand of the war between good and evil. A war that cannot be won unless Christians understand the authority they have in Jesus's name. In view of this, Christians cannot exercise their authority over Satan until they understand how to use the whole armor of God.

We cannot blame all the bad things in the world on Satan. Mankind has played a major role due to disobedience toward God. This disobedience is a combination of our sin nature and free will. Nevertheless, the spiritual war between the forces of good versus evil is responsible for many of the bad things that happen in the world. Despite this, Christians must exercise discernment in situations that clearly show demonic influences. If so, they must use the whole armor of God to remedy the situation. In addition, Christians must realize they war against the flesh and the ways of the world. Still, our chief enemy is Satan. So Christians must walk by faith and not by sight because most of the things we fight against are spiritual and cannot be seen.

Chapter 3

GOD/RELIGION

The dictionary describes God as any of various beings conceived of as supernatural, immortal, and having special powers over the lives and affairs of people and the course of nature. Many Christian theologians would add the words *omnipresent*, *omnipotent*, *always existed*, *creator of the universe*, and *eternal judge of mankind.* Theologians would also include the attributes of God such as love, merciful, long-suffering, patient, kind, and an awarder of those who diligently seek him. If this is God's definition, can anyone question his ways?

If God oversees the universe, then why is there evil in the world? After all, God is all-powerful and knowledgeable. Thus, he can prevent natural disasters from occurring and stop individuals from doing evil acts. Yet God allows mankind to experience the negative effects of evil in the world. Organized religion has different views on the subjects. For example, some religions teach that man cannot question God, while other religions contend that one must accept their plight in life. Conversely, Christianity is a mixture of the two. Yet there are many denominations within Christianity with different views about evil and why God allows it.

There are approximately seven billion people in the world. That is seven billion unique individuals. All these individuals have some belief or concept of God. Even atheists have a belief system—there is no God. In addition, those of faith would agree that God knows our thoughts, heart, and intents. If we concede this point about God, can we question his motives or ways? Furthermore, if God created the universe, his power and majesty is beyond our understanding. Therefore, God must have provided us a means to know him and his laws. I believe the Bible is one of those means.

The Bible has many critics, but they cannot dispute the accuracy of biblical prophecies. For example, many Old Testament prophets predicted future events regarding Israel and its people. Likewise, there are prophetic verses concerning the birth, life, and death of Jesus Christ. For instance, in Isaiah 7:14, we are told details concerning Jesus's birth: "Therefore the Lord Himself will give you a sign: Behold, the virgin shall conceive and bear a Son, and shall call His name Immanuel." Later, in Isaiah 53: 3–7, Jesus's death on the cross is described metaphorically:

> He is despised and rejected by men, A Man of sorrows and acquainted with grief. And we hid, as it were, our faces from Him; He was despised, and we did not esteem Him. Surely He has borne our griefs And carried our sorrows; Yet we esteemed Him stricken, Smitten by God, and afflicted. But He was wounded for our transgressions, He was bruised for our iniquities; The chastisement for our peace was upon Him, And by His stripes we are healed. And we like sheep have gone astray; We have turned, every one, to his own way; And the Lord has laid on Him the iniquity of us all. He was oppressed and He was afflicted, Yet He opened not His mouth; He was led as a lamb to the slaughter, And as a sheep before its shearers is silent, So He opened not his mouth.

These verses were written hundreds of years before Jesus was born. Yet all the symbolic language in these verses refer to Jesus Christ and his death on the cross. Despite this, critics are not convinced the Bible is God's Word.

I believe the greatest evidence for the truthfulness of the Bible—is the Bible. The King James Bible, printed in 1611, was the first widely circulated Bible in the world. Although theologians have different interpretations for Scripture, most agree that the King James version of the Bible served as a template for future versions. On a personal note, I was given a King's James Bible when I joined the army and after I was baptized.

Although the Bible was written by forty different authors, the main spiritual principles are consistent. Man is inherently sinful while God is inherently merciful to those that repent and serve him. We find examples of this in both the New and Old Testament. The story of David illustrates this point. We find in Acts 13:22 a statement from God about David's spiritual potential: "And when He had removed him, He raised up for them David as king, to whom also He gave testimony and said, 'I have found David the son of Jesse, man after My own heart, who will do all My will.'" These verses refer to Saul being removed as king due to his disobedience and God raising up David to be the new king of Israel. Furthermore, God states that David is a man after his own heart. Likewise, Jesus's lineage is through David.

DAVID'S SIN

After Saul dies, David is appointed king. Unlike Saul, David knew God and wanted to serve him with all his heart, mind, and strength. Because of David's faithfulness, God blessed him and the nation of Israel. Unfortunately, after David was well established as a king and man of God, he saw a woman bathing on a rooftop one evening. As a result, he summoned her to his palace even though she was married to one of his military commanders. We find this in 2 Samuel 11:2–5:

> Then it happened one evening that David arose from his bed and walked on the roof of the king's house. And from the roof he saw a woman bathing, and the woman. And someone said, "It this not Bathsheba, the daughter of Eliam, the wife of Uriah the Hittite?" Then David sent messengers, and took her; and she came to him, and he lay with her, for she was cleansed from her impurity; and she returned to her house. And the woman conceived; so she sent and told David, and said, "I am with child."

For many reasons, David could not admit his affair with Bathsheba. So he recalls Bathsheba's husband from the warzone with the intent that he would have sex with his wife. To David's dismay, Uriah refuses to touch his wife or enjoy the comforts of home while his fellow soldiers were fighting on the battlefield. Although David tries his best to persuade Uriah to enjoy his leave from the war front, he does not compromise his convictions. Thus, Uriah gets sent back to the war front. David then writes a letter to his chief military commander (Joab) and informs him to put Uriah at the forefront of the hottest battle and then withdraw from him. Joab does what David requested. Hence, Uriah gets killed in battle. Soon thereafter, David marries Bathsheba. And David believes his problem has been solved. In fact, his actions would have dire consequences for his entire family and the nation of Israel.

The first of these sorrows is the death of Bathsheba's child. Then David's daughter, Tamar, is raped by her brother Amnon. Tamar's brother, Absalom, subsequently murders Amnon because he raped his sister. Later, Absalom leads a rebellion against David. Thus, David must flee for his life by leaving Jerusalem and remain on the run until Absalom is killed. All these events occurred because of David's sin with Bathsheba. David repented and returned to God, but only after Nathan the prophet exposed his sins. Although God showed mercy to David by sparing his life and throne, he still experienced the spiritual consequences for his actions.

The life of David has spiritual lessons for us today. The first lesson is that any Christian can fall into sin if they take their focus off God. Moreover, sinful thoughts that are not confessed will lead to bad results. In David's case, lusting for Bathsheba would not have gotten her pregnant, but acting on those thoughts did. Second, personal sin affects others too. In this situation, Uriah's family suffered the loss of a son and sibling while David would endure tremendous sorrow because of his indiscretion with Bathsheba.

Many Christians know the story of David versus Goliath. It's a great story of faith by one so young. Many of us think back on our faith when we were teenagers, so we're impressed by what David did. Pastors love to preach sermons about David's faith against all odds. To a lesser extent, pastors will preach about David's struggles with Saul and how his faithfulness sustained him in the wilderness. This story is not as popular with pastors as David versus Goliath because the story of David versus Saul involves persecution, ingratitude, jealously, and long-suffering for perceived wrongs. This is not a popular message that believers want to hear.

In addition, pastors avoid sermons concerning David and Bathsheba. They avoid this story because of the spiritual aftermath associated with their affair. In David's situation, his conviction and repentance for his sins did not wipe away the consequences because of them. Hence, there was a cause-and-effect spiritual principle because of his sins. Granted, God will forgive us and restore our fellowship with him if we repent of our sins. Still, when God places one into a position of power and authority such as in ministry or government, personal sin has dire consequences for others too. Since David was the first king of Israel chosen by God, his sins affected the entire nation too.

Many Christians often cite David's life as evidence that God can forgive any sin—even murder. This is true; however, what Christians fail to understand is that David did not escape the consequences for his sins after he repented of them. No, this is not karma. You get what you deserve. However, Christians are not immune from the consequences of their bad actions. And if their actions have violated biblical principles, God will hold them accountable for them. No, this is not an endorsement of hell-and-brimstone sermons about sin and what happens to those that stumble. Instead, it's an understanding of God's requirement that his children be holy—for God is holy. Therefore, Christians must rely on the Holy Spirit to guide them daily to keep their focus on God and his ways.

I do not contend that I know the ways of God. But what I do know is that his ways are not our ways. This is outlined in Isaiah 55:8–9:

> "For My thoughts are not your thoughts, Nor are your ways My ways," says the Lord. "For as the heavens are higher than the earth, So are My ways higher than your ways, And My thoughts than your thoughts."

If one believes that the Bible is the Word of God, then these two verses confirm that no one knows the ways of God. Nevertheless, we can start the process of knowing God by giving our life to Christ and learning to listen to the inner voice of the Holy Spirit. Hence, you're a Christian based on your relationship with Jesus Christ—not on your church attendance or good works. Because good works without faith in God is nothing.

Like David, all Christians make mistakes in life and suffer the consequences because of them. Some of these mistakes won't be life changing, but some will profoundly affect one's life. In view of this, one of the reasons why bad things happen to Christians is due to their bad decisions. Yes, God does forgive us for our sins if we confess them; however, one must still face the consequences for those bad decisions.

For example, a Christian marries a nonbeliever and subsequently experiences marital strife. Although the Christian is faithful and living for the Lord, it's not God's fault if there is strife within the marriage. So any anger or bitterness due to marital problems cannot be directed toward God because this situation was a by-product of a bad decision. Furthermore, if the marriage ends in divorce, one's soul could be wounded. If so, this wound could affect their children too.

DIVORCE CONSEQUENCES

Divorce has devastated our society. The Church too has been crippled by divorce. However, when Christians divorce, they face spiritual consequences too. These consequences involve future relationships of the divorced couple. Likewise, any children of the marriage will experience relationship issues of trust, commitment, and faithfulness to the Word. Although the children of divorced parents have done nothing wrong, they will still experience psychological and spiritual scars because of divorce. These scars will affect their marriages too. Unfortunately, many children of divorce underestimate the effects of it. In view of this, they will often blame future spouses, others, or God when problems arise in their marriages.

Women are especially hurt because of the divorce. Although our society has belittled the importance of marriage, many people still desire to get married. Sadly, when problems arise within marriages today, many people would rather end it than work things out. Likewise, Christians have adopted this same approach. Thus, the divorce rate among Born-Again Christians is the same as that of the culture. This is a by-product of past divorces within Christian families.

The high divorce rate among Christians is also due to spiritual neglect of God's purpose for marriage. In Genesis 2:23–24, we're told why people have a desire to marry and the importance of it:

> And Adam said: "This is now bone of my bones And flesh of my flesh; She shall be called Woman, Because she was taken out of Man." Therefore, a man shall leave

> his father and mother and be joined to his wife, and they shall become one flesh.

Granted, there is a lot of symbolic language here. However, God's purpose for marriage is clear: it's a covenant between a man and woman to serve God as one. Yes, marriage includes physical touch, an emotional connection, and spiritual unity. Yet just getting married because of physical attraction and enjoying fun times together won't sustain a marriage. Because if the spiritual commitment is missing within a marriage, there is nothing to rely on when disagreements and problems arise. In view of this, the Bible provides clear instructions to husbands to reconcile any problems within their marriages. Love your wife as Christ loves the Church. Conversely, wives are to respect their husbands. If Christians obeyed these commands, the divorce rate within the Church would plummet.

Although there is nothing married Christians can do about past divorces within their families, they can exercise discernment and grace toward their spouses. Furthermore, this commitment toward their marriage and God's Word may not be shared by both spouses. In view of this, one cannot be discouraged if their spouse refuses to reciprocate. Unfortunately, men are usually less committed to the marriage than their wives. If so, the wife must be the spiritual leader of the home until her husband matures. Granted, God expects men to be the spiritual leaders of the home, but past wounds may have to be addressed first. Many men have been wounded due to divorces, abuse, neglect, or the absence of male role models while growing up.

Christian women today have heavy burdens to carry. Men expect them to manage the home, address their needs, and work outside the home. These expectations can cause tremendous pressure within marriages. Thus, when husbands are not appreciative of their wives' efforts, the seeds of divorce are planted. Moreover, if the wife is a child of divorce, she may listen and be receptive to the advice of world, flesh, and the devil. To resist these calls for divorce, one must understand the biblical tenets concerning marriage and relationships. This entails more than staying married because God hates divorce.

For a Christian woman to resist the calls for divorce, she must understand that her primary relationship is with Jesus Christ—not her husband. This holds true for men too. A woman, however, values and diligently wants an intimate relationship with her husband. And it's very difficult for a wife to understand that her husband may not want to be as intimate. Granted, God put a desire within women to want closeness with their husbands. Still, the marital covenant is not more important than one's spiritual relationship with God. In short, if God is first place in one's heart, they can embrace and rely on his grace when marital difficulties arise.

Once you've learned to love God with all your heart, mind, and strength, your attitude about behaviors and actions of others will change too. You'll understand and accept that we all fall short of the glory of God. In addition, God will start revealing to you the spiritual reasons for your spouse's behavior. No, God is not going to change your spouse against his or her will. Instead, he'll provide you the grace and compassion to handle any situation. Likewise, God will provide you discernment concerning the psychological, physical, and spiritual reasons why a person acts and does the things they do. This will enable you to be a better spouse and Christian to others, even if they don't want or appreciate your help. As a man who spent twenty years in the military, I can attest that God's grace and mercy is beyond human understanding and reason. Therefore, God's grace is sufficient to survive any bad situation in life.

Relationship issues with spouses or others is the number one reason Christians are angry with God. Hence, many times their children will suffer bad consequences due to their parents' unforgiveness toward others. Although we're Christians, we live in the same world as nonbelievers. As such, we're exposure to the same dark factors as non-Christians. Those factors are the world, flesh, and the enemy. So Christians cannot disobey the Word and expect God's protection—especially if they harbor unforgiveness. In addition, God will provide us discernment if we're obedient about bad situations we're going through in life. Unfortunately, most of our unpleasant experiences are due to our bad decisions or that of others. In view of this, you cannot shake your fist at God when bad things happen to you.

Rather, embrace God's grace and learn to depend on him even when things look bleak.

If you're a Christian, you cannot harbor anger, bitterness, or mistrust toward others or God. Even if the person who hurt you was a parent, family member, or spouse, you must forgive them. No, this is not easy to do, and nonbelievers cannot do it. However, every Christian has access to the Holy Spirit. Thus, what your natural man cannot do, your spiritual man can do. Nevertheless, you must want to get rid of your pain and stop blaming others for it! God does not accept nor does he want to hear your excuses for not forgiving others that hurt you. This is not a debate as to who is right or wrong. Instead, this is a Christian tenet that must be obeyed. Remember, God knows the actions, intents, and words spoken by everyone. So he will be the ultimate judge for what others have done to us. Once you've conceded all judgment to God, you'll sleep better at night.

DISOBEDIENCE

Another biblical law that Christians ignore is their disobedience toward the Word. In short, Christians want to live like nonbelievers but expect God to bless them. When he doesn't, Christians are angry with God when bad things happen to them. Granted, our salvation is based on grace and not of works; however, grace does not mean you're free to disobey God's Word without consequences. True grace is yielding to the Holy Spirit that resides in every true believer.

Unfortunately, many Christians must first be humbled before they yield to the Holy Spirit. A lot of this is due to our free will. Sadly, many Christians believe that going to church and reading their Bible is good enough to please God. In fact, if believers do not learn to love God with all their heart, mind, and strength, those acts won't fulfill them spiritually. Religious activities have the appearance of holiness, but if there is no love for the Word or desire to know God personally, those religious acts won't change them spiritually. Instead, God requires your life, will, and commitment to him.

OLD TESTAMENT LAWS

Many Christian pastors today ignore Old Testament verses concerning judgment and curses for disobedience. They insist that Jesus is the New Covenant. Thus, the commands and tenets of the Old Testament don't apply to Christians. Jesus would disagree with that statement. In fact, Jesus said he came to fulfill the law, not to replace it. Although Jesus's blood sacrifice eliminated animal sacrifices and priestly atonement for our sins, it did not exempt us from bad consequences for willingly disobeying the Word. Likewise, if our governmental leaders disobey the Word, there are consequences for the people they govern. We find many examples of this in the Old Testament. For instance, many kings of Israel brought divine judgment on their nation due to their disobedience. We find many examples of this today in Third World countries where ungodly men rule by fear and corruption.

People throughout history have distorted biblical verses to serve their purposes. Unfortunately, many of these distortions have been used to justify killing people who questioned doctrines taught by the Church or state. Granted, a lot of these distortions occurred in the past when people could not read or have access to bibles. Today, however, we have Christian denominations that are misrepresenting the Word to justify their theology. These denominations insist traditional biblical tenets are outdated, and they need to change with the times. Likewise, they insist the harsh warnings and consequences mentioned in the Old Testament no longer apply due to Jesus's death on the cross. Hence, God is only about love and wanting to make us happy, so we can ignore all the harsh warnings about sin and the consequences because of it.

The truth is that God does not change nor does his ways change. The evidence can be found in Scripture. The Bible is a collection of stories, prophecies, sayings, laws, and principles for individuals and nations to follow. Some of Scripture no longer applies to us directly. Although some commands and laws do not apply to us directly, they still convey spiritual truths. For example, all the commands listed in Leviticus were for the Israelites to obey. There is no argument that some of these laws and commands seemed harsh. However, the blood sacrifice of Jesus did not cover the Israelites. So animal sacrifices along with spiritual laws had to be followed for the people to be right with God. Granted, God is love, but he is holy too and cannot tolerate sin and disobedience. Therefore, without Jesus's blood covering for their sins, Old Testament laws had to be enforced to keep people cleansed before God.

In view of this, quoting verses in Leviticus to chastise Christians guilty of sinful acts distorts Scripture. Yes, God will judge their sin, and there are consequences for their actions. But stoning someone for disobedience would not apply to Christians because of Jesus's atonement for their sins. Conversely, asserting that the warnings and consequences of prohibited acts listed in Leviticus no longer apply to Christians is misleading too. Therefore, whenever you read the Bible, you must always contemplate how verses apply to Christians. If so, you need to discern the spiritual messages within Scripture.

Although much of the Old Testament concerns God's relationship with the Israelites, it's also a preview of his character and ways. The Old Testament clearly shows that God is holy, and he expects his children to be obedient too. But Scripture also shows that God knows man cannot be holy without blood atonement. In addition, God provides plenty of wisdom and instruction throughout the Old Testament to keep us focused on him. For example, in the books of Proverbs and Psalms, there are insightful verses that provide wisdom and instructions for living. Although these instructions were given to the Israelites, they apply to Christians too.

Many pastors often cite Deuteronomy 28:1–14 because it reveals all the blessings you receive for being obedient to the Word. However, pastors won't elaborate on the negative consequences for being disobedient to the Word. These warnings are listed in Deuteronomy 28:15–68. In these verses, God clearly details all the pitfalls of disobedience. No, this is not confirmation that God is ready to pounce on you for doing wrong. Instead, God is warning his children to avoid certain behaviors or acts that could cause them harm. Since God is the ultimate father, he must be both stern and loving toward his children.

The blessings and curses listed in Deuteronomy chapter 28 still apply to us today, even though some of these verses seem harsh and not pertinent to Christians. Despite this, the biblical tenets listed in Deuteronomy chapter 28 must be understood and complied with. In Deuteronomy 28:1–6, we are told the initial blessings from God for obedience:

> Now it shall come to pass, if you diligently obey the voice of the Lord your God, to observe carefully all His commandments which I command you today, that the Lord your God will set you high above all nations of the earth. And all these blessings shall come upon you and overtake you, because you obey the voice of the Lord your God: Blessed shall you be in the city, and blessed shall you be in the country. Blessed shall be the fruit of your body, the produce of your ground and the increase of your herds, the increase of your cattle and the offspring of your flocks. Blessed shall be your basket and your kneading bowl. Blessed shall you be when you come in, and blessed shall you be when you go out.

In contrast, we find in Deuteronomy 28:15–19 the initial curses for being disobedience:

> But it shall come to pass, if you do not obey the voice of the Lord your God, to observe carefully all His commandments and His statutes which I command you today, that all these curses will come upon you and overtake you: Cursed shall you be in the city, and cursed shall you be in

> the country. Cursed shall be your basket and your kneading bowl. Cursed shall be the fruit of your body and the produce of your land, the increase of your cattle and offspring of your flocks. Cursed shall you be when you come in, and cursed shall you be when you go out.

Although these verses were meant for the Israelites of the Old Testament, God is revealing spiritual blessings for obedience and consequences for disobedience. In addition, a lot of the language used in Deuteronomy chapter 28, is symbolic. Even though a lot of these curses were meant for the Israelites, they also convey spiritual consequences that apply to Christians today. The main spiritual consequence is disobedience to God's Word has repercussions. Thus, even if one repents of known sin, there may still be repercussions because of it. Reason for this: repentance does not cancel consequences.

SUMMATION

The premise of this book is that factors can be weighed and predict results. Therefore, there must be God factors too that can be weighed and predict possible results. Granted, God is beyond human understanding. In view of this, no human model based on factors can explain the ways of God. Nevertheless, a model based on biblical laws and principles can reveal possible reasons why bad things to happen to good people. These reasons may not be logical to us, yet God clearly shows us throughout the Bible that his ways are not our ways.

Disobedience to God's Word is not a popular sermon today. Most people attend church to be uplifted and supported by others, so sermons that tear them down won't produce the desired effect. However, sermons that reveal and instruct members about the consequences of disobedience must be preached. This message coupled with God's unconditional love for people can change lives. Because if people realize that God desires an intimate relationship with them, this truth can radically change them. Unfortunately, most churches today have turned away from their first love. That first love is Jesus Christ. In view of this, churches must go back to the basics of Christianity. The basics start with showing genuine concern and compassion toward hurting people searching for answers.

For this to occur, Christians must be committed to Jesus Christ. If they are committed to Jesus Christ, they will love God and learn to love others too. If followed, when nonbelievers or carnal Christians experience bad things, strong believers can encourage them and show them God's grace. The church has no choice; it must do this to counter evil in the world because bad things will continue to happen to good people. Although many bad events occur due to poor decisions by people, sometimes there are no answers to explain why. Despite this, God's love can heal all wounds.

As Christians, we must be honest with people. In view of this, when loved ones or friends suffer due to disobedience to God's Word, we don't judge them. Nevertheless, if they ask us why God allowed this to happen to them, we must be honest and show them Scripture if it applies to their situation. For example, your daughter has sex outside of marriage and gets pregnant or contracts a STD (sexually transmitted disease). Do we blame the young man for this result? Although he is not innocent, the answer is no. Because most Christians know that sex outside of marriage is wrong. Yet many Christian men and women disobey this biblical tenet concerning sexual purity prior to marriage.

In Ephesians 5:31, we are told about the marriage covenant: "For this reason a man shall leave his father and mother and be joined to his wife, and the two shall become one flesh." This covenant is more than a spiritual connection. It's a physical and emotional oneness too. In view of this, all three parts of this oneness must be present within a marriage. Thus, when men and women have sex prior to marriage, they lose that physical oneness that God intended. When this occurs, it can cause intimacy issues within the marriage. Because those previous sexual relationships have left spiritual scars that must to be healed. Likewise, the Bible says that when a man joins with a harlot, they become one flesh (1 Corinthians 6:16 says, "Or do you not know that he who is joined to a harlot is one body with her? For the two, He says, shall become one flesh."). This verse is telling us that physical sex affects people spiritually and emotionally.

There are many reasons for the decline of the family in America today. The sexual revolution of the sixties is one of those reasons. This movement changed how our culture viewed sex prior to marriage. This affected Christians too. Because Christians started rejecting what the Bible teaches about sexual purity prior to marriage. Hence, when believers are involved in physical relationships prior to marriage, they get scarred emotionally and spiritually. This is especially true for women. So even though Christians are waiting to get married, this has not changed the divorce rate among believers, mainly because Christians still expect their spouses to obey the Word concerning marriage. For women, this means that men must love their wives like Christ loves the church, while men expect their wives to respect them as husbands.

In view of this, if you have suffered through a divorce or experienced many failed relationships, there is nothing you can do to change the past. What you can do is renew your mind and heart by releasing your pain to God. As a Christian, you know that you're a new creation created in God's image. Therefore, feed that new image by living the life God intended you to live. So whether you're a sole-parent mother or woman who has suffered a devastating divorce, don't blame God for your pain. Even if you've been a model wife and mother and have done nothing wrong, you must realize that others have disobeyed God's Word. Therefore, you cannot be bitter toward others or God. In addition, you must forgive them and rely on God's grace to move forward.

Christians have a bad habit of citing Scripture to people when they are down or have sinned. Despite this, knowing your Bible and how the Word applies to given situations can provide you hope. In Romans 5:1–5, we are given a battle plan to address our troubles.

> Therefore, having been justified by faith, we have peace with God through our Lord Jesus Christ, through whom also we have access by faith into the grace in which we stand, and rejoice in hope of the glory of God. And not only that, but we also glory in tribulations, knowing that tribulations produces perseverance; and perseverance, character; and character, hope. Now hope does not disappoint, because the love of God has been poured out in our hearts by the Holy Spirit who was given to us.

If all Christians could learn to depend on God during difficult times, our world would change overnight.

Biblical disobedience is undermining the Church. As Christians, we must realize that open disobedience to God's Word has repercussions. Although this seems harsh, the Bible should not be viewed as a rule book. Instead, it's God's spiritual guide to avoid behaviors that undermine our faith. Although there are many acts of disobedience by Christians today, sexual disobedience is the one that has devastated families and individuals. Therefore, for this trend to change, Christians must learn to honor God with both body and mind. This will not be easy given our promiscuous culture. However, by yielding and trusting to the inner voice of Holy Spirit, you will have the strength to walk away from sinful desires.

Clearly, disobedience to God's Word has consequences that can be measured. And the Bible clearly warns us that sinful acts have consequences. Most Christians understand that obvious sins such as adultery, stealing, false witness, or murder can lead to bad things. What many Christians don't understand are the biblical warnings concerning what we say, think, or believe. In 2 Corinthians 10:3–5, we are told that all struggles are spiritual:

> For though we walk in the flesh, we do not war according to the flesh. For the weapons

> of our warfare are not carnal but mighty in God for pulling down strongholds, casting down arguments and every high thing that exalts itself against the knowledge of God, bringing every thought into captivity to the obedience of Christ.

These verses provide us spiritual clues of the forces against Christians. They also tell us how to live godly in a fallen world.

Although the enemy is responsible for many of the bad things that happen to Christians, our actions often give him permission to attack us. Most Christians realize that physical acts of disobedience have spiritual consequences. What is harder for Christians to admit, and repent of, are the hidden sins of the disobedience. Sins like bitterness, unforgiveness, pride, and legalism have devastated the Church. And many Christians are unaware of these sins or refuse to repent of them. In Hebrews 12:15, we are warned about hidden sins: "Looking carefully lest anyone fall short of the grace of God; lest any root of bitterness springing up cause trouble, and by this many become defiled." This verse is short, yet it warns us of dire consequences for disobeying this tenet.

Granted, Satan is responsible for many of the negative consequences of hidden sins. Yet we give him the right to inflict us because of our unconfessed sins. In view of this, by violating God's command by not forgiving others, we trigger spiritual consequences that God cannot stop until we repent. Moreover, if we have harbored ill feelings toward someone for many years, the spiritual effects don't get blotted out easily. Nevertheless, Christians must clean the slate with God and the parties that harmed them to move forward.

All the sorrows of mankind are caused by neglect or open disobedience to Scripture. In view of this, when you experience hardship or loss in life, a spiritual inventory of your life is necessary. Be frank with your assessment. Also, be receptive to possible God factors that caused your situation. These factors are not always obvious. Still, if you sincerely seek the Lord on this matter, Scripture compels God to answer you. Remember, God's timing and ways are not your timing and ways. Nevertheless, when you learn to trust God and his ways, the sorrows of this world cannot compare to his grace. Amazing grace, how sweet it is. Once you get it, it will change your life forever.

Chapter 4

HIS MYSTERIOUS WAYS

Many people are familiar with the adage "his mysteries ways." This adage refers to the amazing ways in which God works things out for people. Books on the subject are very popular. Likewise, there are Christian magazines that solely write stories about God's supernatural ways. These stories always have happy conclusions. Conversely, these magazines do not write articles about unanswered prayers. Even though all Christians have been frustrated with God due to unanswered prayers, yet we enthusiastically praise God for answered prayers, but choose to ignore him for unanswered prayers. Despite this contradiction, most Christians know there were reasons why their prayers were not answered.

Unanswered prayers frustrate many Christians. Furthermore, Christian denominations have different views concerning unanswered prayers. For example, they differ on why we pray and how to do it. For instance, Catholics believe that Mary (Jesus's mother) is the intercessor for their prayers. Protestants insist that only Jesus can answer prayers. Although most Protestant denominations believe that Christians must pray in Jesus's name, they disagree on why we pray and for what. In addition, many clergymen have personal beliefs concerning prayers, which they convey to their churches. Therefore, there is no consensus within the Church concerning prayer.

Jesus's disciples had questions about praying. So they asked him how should they pray. In Luke 11:2–4, Jesus provides them an answer:

> So He said to them, "When you pray, say: 'Our Father in heaven, Hallowed be Your name. Your kingdom come. Your will be done On earth as it is in heaven. Give us day by day our daily bread. And forgive us our sins, for we also forgive everyone who is indebted to us. And do not lead us into temptation, But deliver us from the evil one.'"

When I attended Catholic school as a youth, I had to memorize these verses; however, I did not fully understand what these verses meant.

Mature believers recognize that Jesus in these verses is revealing how to live the Christian life. The key word is *will*—not our will but God's. In short, we are to obey God's plan for our lives and live as ambassadors for Christ. This is important because God never intended for the world to be ruled by dark forces. In addition, the goal and purpose for our lives is not about gain and fame. Instead, it's about service to God and others. And while we pursue that life, if others subsequently hurt or misuse us, we are to forgive them. Although we don't have to trust people who hurt us, we must forgive them.

The final point of Jesus's words about prayer in Luke 11:2–4 involves temptation and how to avoid it. For Christians to avoid temptation, they must rely on the inner voice of the Holy Spirit to guide them. If they don't, they can be ensnared by the same dark forces that affect nonbelievers. That snare is our sin nature. Hence, if a Christian's sin nature controls them, they will lose faith in God. Once a Christian loses their faith in God, they will lose all hope for the future too.

For a Christian to avoid this spiritual state, they must be obedient to the Word by staying connected to God via the Holy Spirit. This is a spiritual process that takes time and commitment by the believer. For a Christian to lean on the Holy Spirit, they must surrender their will to God's. Unfortunately, many Christians never learn how to surrender their will to God's. As a result, they are frustrated, fearful, and angry that God does not bless them or answer their prayers.

This frustration within the Church has caused many Christians to pursue unbiblical answers for their problems. As a result, believers are searching for answers to their problems via prosperity preachers, positive thinking gurus, or psychics because they are seeking quick fixes and answers to serious problems. They pursue these false hopes because they don't understand God's purpose for prayer.

In James 4:3, we are told about praying for the wrong reasons: "You ask, and do not receive, because you ask amiss, that you may spend it on your pleasures." Granted, many Christians pray for physical and mental healings for loved ones and self. These are sincere prayers that God hears, and he understands our suffering and that of others. Although these prayers are sincere, there may be spiritual reasons why God cannot answer their prayers the way they want. God is not Santa Claus. Our prayers are not meant to be a wish list. Instead, they are meant to strengthen our relationship with God as we do his will. Remember, God knows your needs. Yet we must wait on him to fulfill those needs. In Matthew 10:30–31, Jesus provides us a mental picture to focus on when we doubt God's love for us: "But the very hairs of your head are all numbered. Do not fear therefore; you are of more value than many sparrows."

The Church is often referred to as the Body of Christ. So if some parts of that body are sick, it affects the entire body. If Christians are told that Jesus expects them to claim financial prosperity and success, they won't respond well to adversity. Likewise, if they expect to be happy and joyful 24/7, feelings of sadness and disappointment will diminish their faith in God. Unfortunately, this prosperity message has permeated the Christian Church. Sadly, when believers don't experience the success and happiness promised to them by their pastors, they drift away and become bitter toward God.

To reverse this negative trend within the Church, Christians must return to the basics of faith. The basics of faith is that Jesus died on the cross for our sins to restore our relationship with the Father. Therefore, as Christians, we live our lives by relying on the Holy Spirit to guide us. Although we live in the world, we are not of the world. In short, we cannot live like the devil and expect God's favor. If we live for God, he will provide for our needs. Those needs are not our wants. Furthermore, when perceived bad things happen to us, God is aware of our situation. Thus, we pray for strength, wisdom, and perseverance to do God's will regardless of the forces against us. In short, if God is for us, no one can stand against us.

CHOSEN PEOPLE

People of faith believe that God is fair, so the thought that God would show favor toward unworthy people frustrates many Christians. Despite this, the Bible seems to support that certain unworthy people get blessed due to the righteous of a few. We find proof of this within the stories of the Bible. In these stories, God blesses individuals because of their faithfulness. As a result, their family and nation get blessed too—even though these individuals have done nothing worthy of blessings. This spiritual tenet puzzles many Christians, even though Christians know their salvation is not based on good works, but by the blood sacrifice of Jesus Christ for humanity. A gift that humanity did not deserve.

The first example of this can be found in the book of Genesis. We are told that God regrets creating mankind. Hence, he decides to destroy humanity except for Noah and his family. In Genesis 6:5–8, we are told how God feels about mankind:

> Then the Lord saw that the wickedness of man was great in the earth, and that every intent of the thoughts of his heart was only evil continually. And the Lord was sorry that

> He had made man on the earth, and He was grieved in His heart. So the Lord said, "I will destroy man whom I have created from the face of the earth, both man and beast, creeping thing and birds of the air, for I am sorry that I have made them." But Noah found grace in the eyes of the Lord.

The Bible does not elaborate on why Noah found favor with God. We are just told that Noah walked with God.

Besides Noah, God spares his wife, sons, and their wives, even though there is no indication that Noah's household was righteous before God. Nevertheless, God spares them because of Noah's righteous. The Bible only provides us one clue concerning the righteous of Noah's sons. This is recorded in Genesis 9:20–23:

> And Noah began to be a farmer, and he planted a vineyard. Then he drank of the wine and was drunk, and became uncovered in his tent. And Ham, the father of Canaan, saw the nakedness of his father, and told his two brothers outside. But Shem and Japheth took a garment, laid it on both their shoulders, and went backward and covered the nakedness of their father. Their faces were turned away, and they did not see their father's nakedness. So Noah awoke from his wine, and knew what his younger son had done to him.

Clearly these verses reveal the spiritual condition of Ham versus that of his brothers. As a result, Ham gets cursed by Noah while his other sons get blessed.

If Noah was the most righteous person on the earth before and after the flood, then why would he curse Ham for this one act of disrespect? No doubt there was more to Ham's spiritual condition then we know. Thus, was Ham worthy to be spared from the flood while children throughout the world were drowned? If not, why would God destroy young children but allow Ham to survive the flood?

Granted, we are not told why God did not spare young children from the flood. In view of this, we must concede that God knew the future spiritual state of all these children. If so, God's judgment toward these children was rendered based on the spiritual factors pertaining to their parents. If true, then faithful and righteous parents may influence or prevent God from punishing disobedient children with eternal consequences. Nevertheless, they will still experience consequences for their sinful acts.

After Noah, God then establishes a covenant with a man named Abram, which we know as Abraham. Again, we are not told in Scripture why God considers Abraham to be righteous and worthy of blessings. What we are told are the instructions and promises given to Abraham by God. This is found in Genesis 12:1–3:

> Now the lord had said to Abram: "Get out of your country, From your family And from your father's house, To a land that I will show you. I will make you a great nation; I will bless you And make your name great; And you shall be a blessing. I will bless those who bless you, And I will curse him who curses you; And in you all the families of the earth shall be blessed."

Abraham was promised the land of Canaan, which is modern-day Israel, even though other people controlled Canaan during this time. Yet God tells Abraham that his descendants will have this land. Furthermore, this land transfer would not be a peaceful transition; it would be taken by force centuries later by the Israelites—Abraham's descendants. So the perceived rights of the people that lived in Canaan did not deter God from promising this land to Abraham's descendants. In view of this, we must concede that God decides matters based on his laws and principles—not that of man's.

In addition to the land of Canaan, God also promised Abraham two other things that would impact biblical history. The second promise is mentioned in Genesis 13:16: "And I will make your descendants as the dust of the earth; so that if a man could number the dust of the earth, then your descendants also could be numbered." The third promise was that Abraham would have a son with his wife Sarah. This is recorded in Genesis 17:19: "Then God said: 'No, Sarah your wife shall bear you a son, and you shall call his name Isaac; I will establish My covenant with him for an everlasting covenant, and with his descendants after him.'" Although Abraham had a son by the name of Ishmael, God's covenant would be established through Sarah's son.

Many theologians believe God's reference to Abraham's descendants includes Christians. New Testament Scripture seems to support this position. Paul presents this point when he was a prisoner in Rome. In Romans 11:17–18, Paul explains how the Gentiles are now part of God's covenant:

> And if some of the branches were broken off, and you, being a wild olive tree, were grafted in among them, and with them became a partaker of the root and fatness of the olive tree, do not boast against the branches. But if you do boast, remember that you do not support the root, but the root supports you.

The root in these verses is symbolic for God; moreover, Christians are righteous before God because of the blood sacrifice of Jesus Christ because Jesus Christ established a new covenant. A covenant that anyone can enter if they accept Christ as their savior.

Many people question God's fairness for blessing Israel because of Abraham's righteousness. Yet they ignore God's subsequent forgiveness of sin through the blood sacrifice of Jesus Christ—a gift that humanity did not deserve. In view of this, the argument that God is unfair because of his first covenant with Israel is a moot point because the righteousness of one man blessed many in both covenants. In addition, there were eternal consequences for the Israelites who rejected the Abrahamic Covenant and for those who reject Christ as the New Covenant.

CALLED

This spiritual tenet of God blessing many due to the righteousness of one still applies to us today. Granted, we don't have great men of faith like Noah or Abraham inspiring us to live Godly. Instead, we have Jesus's atonement for our sins, which provides access to God via the Holy Spirit for believers. In short, every Christian can have the same intimate relationship with God as did Noah, Abraham, and all the Old Testament prophets. The only reason a believer would not have an intimate relationship with God is because of unbelief, doubt, disobedience, or idols. An idol is anything a person places more faith in than God. I believe this point is confirmed in Matthew 20:16: "So the last will be first, and the first last. For many are called, but few chosen."

God still chooses people today. Yes, a lot of these chosen people are meant for ministry; however, many more are chosen to change eternal destinies for their family. On a personal note, I was the first member of my family to be Born Again. And because of my decision for Christ, other family members came to Christ years later. In addition, my children were brought up in a Christian home. Thus, this spiritual domino effect changed the eternal destiny of my family. Furthermore, although I've been a Christian for almost forty years now, I still have no idea why God saved me. But because he did, I touched members of my family and others too.

There are times in history when God must intervene in the affairs of mankind. When these times occur, God uses people to fulfill his purposes. For example, Christianity no longer appeals to young people in the United States, mainly because their parents were not active Christians. Thus, millennials have been shaped by the culture, a culture that mocks Christianity. If this trend continues, the United States will become a secular society, like Europe. In view of this, I believe that God will be calling people to change the eternal destinies of their family members and friends. And unlike previous generations, I believe many millennials will lead their parents to salvation. If so, they will experience ridicule and repercussions from family and friends. Nevertheless, like Old Testament prophets, they must stay the course.

We are not told in the Bible why God chooses certain people for his purposes. However, what is clear is that those whom God chooses will suffer repercussions. Those repercussions may not be bodily harm, but could be verbal attacks from family and friends. Yes, being chosen is a factor that can be weighed. So if you're experiencing attacks based on your faith, this is a spiritual factor. The Bible warns us that we'll have trouble in this world. Therefore, personal attacks for doing God's work should be expected.

FREE WILL

The belief in free will has puzzled mankind since creation. Likewise, free will has caused a lot of hardship for humanity. Despite this, most people want to make their own decisions, although many times those decisions lead to bad results. And when they lead to bad results, often people want to blame others for those consequences. No doubt our culture has shaped how people view their bad decisions; nevertheless, this does not excuse individual responsibility for them. This also applies to whether one wants to have faith in God and belief in the afterlife.

If free will can make us choose bad things that affect our future and that of others, why did God give it to us? Because based on human history, we have not done a good job with free will. Nevertheless, God intended for humanity to be one with him and prosper on earth. This is recorded in Genesis 1:26–27:

> Then God said, "Let Us make man in Our image, according to Our likeness; let them have dominion over the fish of the sea, over the birds of the air, and over the cattle, over all the earth and over every creeping thing that creeps on the earth." So God created man in His own image; in the image of God He created him; male and female He created them.

We find in Genesis 2:16–17 God's introduction of free will:

> And the Lord God commanded the man, saying, "Of every tree of the garden you may freely eat; but of the tree of the knowledge of good and evil you shall not eat, for in the day that you eat of it you shall surely die."

Unfortunately, Satan tricked Eve into eating the forbidden fruit. Thus, Adam and Eve are expelled from the Garden by God because of their disobedience. The sin of disobedience breaks man's intimate relationship with God. Although God would later establish another covenant with humanity through Abraham, it did not change human nature, a nature that opposes the ways of God. In view of this, humanity needed a savior to cover their sins and restore their relationship with God.

CHRISTIANITY

Christians believe that Jesus Christ was that savior, and for two thousand years, Europeans have embraced Christianity. As a result, Christianity became the dominant religion in Europe and throughout the Western World. Although that is still true today, church attendance has declined significantly in Europe since the end of World War II. In countries like Sweden, Norway, and Demark, only 5 to 7 percent of the population attend church, whereas in countries like France, Germany, and Spain, less than 20 percent attend church. In predominant Catholic countries like Italy, Ireland, and Poland, the numbers are higher; however, they too have been declining for years. Granted, church attendance does not confirm the number of Christians in a country, but it does provide information on the type of Christian churches that people attend and how strongly they influence the culture of that country.

Church attendance has declined in the United States too; however, almost 50 percent of Americans still attend church regularly. Yet many American Christians are becoming apathetic toward church and the importance of it. In many ways, Americans are embracing the same attitudes and perception of Christianity shared by the culture. For example, one common excuse for not going to church is that people who attend are hypocrites. If a hypocrite is someone who says one thing but does another, there is truth to that statement. However, if a person attends church because they are struggling with immorality, then attending services is important for them emotionally and spiritually. One cannot argue one point without conceding the other.

Conversely, many Christians who attend church regularly are strong believers that can provide support and wisdom for people struggling with their faith. In Proverbs 27:17, we get confirmation that people need to be uplifted by others: "As iron sharpens iron, so a man sharpens the countenance of his friend." Even secular psychology recognizes that people need love and support from others.

This decline in church attendance in the United States is especially alarming among millennials. Even millennials with strong Christian upbringings are falling away from the church. There are many reasons why young adults do not attend church. The first reason is because their parents did not attend church. So although they may have attended church as children through bus ministries, if their parents did not attend with them, they lost interest as teenagers. Another reason is that millennials find church boring and unfulfilling. Sadly, there is truth to this statement. Many Christian churches today are focusing on an entertainment experience instead of praise and worship services. Conversely, some churches are dead spiritually, and there is no movement of the Holy Spirit among its members.

As an exception, churches affiliated with the Charismatic or Pentecostal movement are growing while Catholic and mainstream Protestant churches are losing members—especially millennials. People are joining these types of churches because they emphasize the supernatural gifts of the Holy Spirit. The pastors of these churches are proclaiming the gifts of the Holy Spirit such as speaking in tongues, laying hands on the sick, and casting off demons. And these gifts are being given to believers today because of Jesus's imminent return for his Church. Likewise, these gifts are to be used to deliver people from demonic oppression. Although the growth of these churches is undeniable, many Protestant denominations are skeptical of the doctrines being taught by these churches.

In 2 Thessalonians 2:3, we are told about a sign that will precede the rise of the Antichrist: "Let no one deceive you by any means, for that Day will not come unless the falling away comes first, and the man of sin is revealed, the son of perdition." This verse pertains to the strength of the Christian Church in the world prior to the rise of the Antichrist. Conversely, we find in Acts 2:17 an outpouring of the Holy Spirit throughout the world: "'And it shall come to pass in the last days,' says God, 'That I will pour out of My Spirit on all flesh; Your sons and daughters shall prophesy, Your young men shall see visions, Your old men shall dream dreams.'" Again, this pertains to a period prior to the rise of the Antichrist. I believe both verses pertain to the same period in history. Thus, many Christians during this time will become apathetic toward the Word, while some believers and new converts will experience an outpouring of the Holy Spirit.

There is little doubt that traditional Christianity is under attack by the culture. Nevertheless, Christians have a choice to live by the spiritual principles of the Bible or give in to the norms of the culture. Granted, some Christian churches are compromising biblical principles to appease their members and the culture. Despite this, that is not justification for Christians to comply with these practices. All

Christians have free will to obey or disregard Scripture. In view of this, when Christians walk away from biblical principles and engage in activities they know are wrong, they set in motion bad consequences. Spiritual apathy is one of these consequences.

Spiritual apathy is a negative factor of free will. Because once a believer becomes apathetic to the things of God, they can be tempted by activities that will destroy their testimony for Christ. Despite this, true believers won't be trapped by sin indefinitely that dishonors God. Therefore, once they repent of their sin, God will welcome them back into his fellowship. Still, their decision to disobey God for a season could have dire consequences. No, this is not God punishing them for their disobedience, but it's God allowing natural and spiritual factors to run their course. God is holy, and he won't keep us from suffering bad consequences due to our mistakes. In short, God allows this suffering to shape our spiritual character. Although many prosperity pastors dispute this spiritual cause and effect principle, their position contradicts Scripture.

The main theme of this book is that bad things happen to good people because of known and unknown factors. I contend our stubborn free will is responsible for many of the bad things that happen to us in life. Hence, when no other factor can be cited when we suffer from a bad event, free will may be the culprit. In the Bible, Paul proclaims that we are at war with our flesh. We find this in Romans 7:15: "For what I am doing, I do not understand. For what I will to do, that I do not practice; but what I hate, that I do." Although this verse refers to the struggle Christians face daily between mind and spirit, it also applies to our daily decisions. In view of this, when we give in to our fleshly desires and ignore the warnings of the Holy Spirit, we set in motion forces that can cause bad things to happen. Granted, there are many factors to assess when bad things happen to us. Nevertheless, if our bad choice or free will was the deciding factor for the result, the blame falls on us.

Chapter 5

GOD'S WARNINGS

Many Christians are familiar with the adage "Wait on the Lord." Even though this is often cited when prayers are not answered quickly, there is more to this adage than unanswered prayers. God knows your needs, and he is your provider. Yet your needs cannot be your desires. So if your desires are to please self, God is not obligated to grant your prayer requests. In addition, there could be spiritual impediments that are preventing God from answering your prayers. These spiritual impediments are activities or wrong pursuits that consume your time and attention. Sadly, many Christians are only concerned about what Jesus can do for them. As a result, they are only interested in getting things from God, but not willing to serve him and do what he expects from them.

In view of this, what does God expect from Christians? The short answer is that he expects them to conform to the image of Jesus Christ. This is a lifelong process, not a goal that can be achieved given our fallen nature. If this goal cannot be achieved, why pursue it? We pursue it because in the process, we will use the talents and abilities God has given us to do his work. For example, some Christians are meant to be in full-time ministry while others are to support them. That support includes all the people behind a pastor or ministry. Although we may not understand how our role supports others, God knows how it does. Our job is to be obedient to what he calls us to do. And sometimes, that role could simply be to take an interest in someone that no one else can reach for Christ.

The Church has millions of members throughout the world. Although many share similar backgrounds and paths to Christ, they all have unique stories behind their testimonies. Given this uniqueness within the Church, not every believer has been trained to research Scripture for answers. Likewise, many Christians do not understand how to listen or be receptive to the voice of the Holy Spirit. Thus, just attending church and reading their bibles won't be enough for them to grow spiritually. Also, there may be unknown factors such as generational curses and judgments, demonic strongholds, and unconfessed sin that keeps them from growing spiritually. In view of this, God will use unconventional ways to speak to believers. One of these unconventional ways is dreams.

DREAMS

The dictionary definition of a dream is a series of images or thoughts in the mind of a person asleep. No doubt you have asked the question that I have asked many times: Why did I have that dream? Often our dreams are due to stressful situations we're going through. Stress at work, concerns for our children or spouse, or unforeseen events are all possible explanations for a dream or series of dreams.

One may also experience disturbing dreams after watching some violent or explicit movies. Most of us, though, have learned to connect the proverbial dots between vivid dreams and something we watched or experienced. There are times though when those dots cannot be connected. When those times occur, we are left wondering about our disturbing dreams.

Dreams and trying to understand those dreams are two common experiences that all people share. And throughout the ages, people have written about and tried to explain why we dream. Despite all the research and study of dreams throughout history, one thing remains true: dreams are mysterious. Dreams are mysteries because they cannot easily be explained. That fact along with the personal nature of our dreams is the reason we ponder the question, Is God behind our dreams?

No doubt you can recall a dream from your past that was vivid and unforgettable. And you asked the question, Was that dream from God? If so, how would you discern the meaning of that dream? There is a book that has a lot to say about dreams. That book is the Bible. One verse that speaks to our times loud and clear is Acts 2:17: "And it shall come to pass in the last days, says God, that I will pour out my Spirit on all flesh: Your sons and daughters shall prophesy, your young men shall see visions, your old men shall dream dreams." By any interpretation, the Lord is not speaking about normal dreams here.

The Bible is the most powerful book ever written and the most mysterious book ever written as well. Mysterious in the sense that God does not fully explain why he does what he does. But when God reveals the same message in both the Old and New Testament, then it applies to us today as well. For example, no one can argue that the acts of stealing, murder, and adultery were cited in both testaments and are still considered sinful practices by God today. So can we use the same rationale for controversial topics such as hearing from God via dreams?

In the Bible, there are many passages concerning dreams. God used dreams throughout the Bible to communicate his will. Some biblical dreams were warnings, while others were instructions. In addition, we find in the books of Genesis and Daniel prophecy dreams to Joseph and the king of Babylon. God spoke to both people of faith and the ungodly through dreams. Furthermore, after these individuals experienced their spiritual dreams, they were prompted to change course because of them.

Most of the dreams cited in the Bible are in the Old Testament. Although in the Book of Matthew, we find that Joseph, the Three Kings, and Pilate's wife experienced spiritual dreams too. The only other dream of note in the New Testament is listed in Acts 2:17: "'And it shall come to pass in the last days,' says God, 'That I will pour out My Spirit on all flesh; Your sons and your daughters shall prophesy, Your young men shall see visions, Your old men shall dream dreams.'" The key phrase in this verse is "My Spirit." God's Spirit is the Holy Spirit. So receiving messages from God via prophesies, visions, or dreams are the work of the Holy Spirit.

Although the earliest books of the Bible were written thousands of years ago, God's laws, principles, and tenets still apply to us today. One reason the Bible applies to us today can be found in Hebrews 4:12: "For the word of God is living and powerful, and sharper than any two-edged sword, piercing even to the division of soul and spirit, and of joints and marrow, and is a discerner of the thoughts and intents of the heart." This passage reveals why people are changed once they apply God's Word to their lives.

If Scripture is truly living and powerful, then verses concerning dreams apply to us today. Matter of fact, God used dreams throughout the Bible for different purposes, but there was one common reason for these dreams: to change course. This change course message within biblical dreams covered many different subjects: warnings from God, deception by others, battle plans, and spiritual errors were all reasons why God intervened through dreams in the affairs of people. In view of this, by studying the dreams of the Bible, we can understand how they apply to us today.

BIBLICAL DREAMS

In Genesis 20: 3–7, we find a warning dream with deception:

> But God came to Abimelech in a dream by night, and said to him, "Indeed you are a dead man because of the woman whom you have taken, for she is a man's wife." But Abimelech had not come near her; and he said, "Lord, will You slay a righteous nation also? Did he not say to me, She is my sister? And she, even she herself said, He

> is my brother. In the integrity of my heart and innocence of my hands I have done this." And God said to him in a dream, "Yes, I know that you did this in the integrity of your heart. For I also withheld you from sinning against Me; therefore I did not let you touch her. Now therefore, restore the man's wife; for he is prophet, and he will pray for you and you shall live. But if you do not restore her, know that you shall surely die, you an all who are yours."

BACKDROP

This event occurred after Abraham separated from Lot and settled in a place called Gerar. Prior to entering Gerar, Abraham decided to tell the people there that Sarah was his sister. Abraham did this because Sarah was beautiful, and he felt that if men knew that she was his wife, they would kill him. Because of this deception, when King Abimelech saw Sarah, he wanted her. As a result, he took her to his household because he thought that Sarah was Abraham's sister. And Abimelech assumed that Abraham would agree to give him Sarah for a price.

This dream demonstrated both God's character and holiness. It also confirmed that God's purposes will be fulfilled even when his children failed to show faith in him. In this situation, Abraham failed to trust God for his protection in this new land. Despite this failure, Abraham went on to become the "Father of Faith." This story is a spiritual lesson to remember that God is merciful and patient with his children. Conversely, this story also shows us that God will speak to the ungodly when they threaten his children or purposes. Since God is the ultimate judge, he knew that Abimelech's actions were done with integrity. So he spared any consequences against Abimelech once he returned Sarah back to Abraham.

In Genesis 37:5–7, we find a prophesy dream for Joseph:

> Now Joseph had a dream, and he told it to his brothers; and they hated him even more. So he said to them, "Please hear this dream which I have dreamed: There we were, binding sheaves in the field. Then behold, my sheaf arose and also stood upright; and indeed your sheaves stood all around and bowed down to my sheaf."

Then in Genesis 37:9, Joseph gets confirmation that his previous dream was from God:

> Then he dreamed still another dream and told it to his brothers, and said, "Look, I have dreamed another dream. And this time, the sun, the moon, and the eleven starts bowed down to me."

BACKDROP

Jacob was the patriarch of Israel and father of twelve sons. The descendants of these sons became the twelve tribes of Israel. Before Jacob was married or had any children, he decided to work for his uncle Laban so he could marry his daughter Rachael, whom he loved. Jacob agreed to work for seven years to marry Rachael. After he worked those seven years for Rachael, Laban arranged a great marriage feast for Jacob; however, Laban decided to trick Jacob on his wedding night by sending him his eldest daughter Leah instead of Rachael. The next day, Jacob was upset because he had been tricked. Laban, therefore, agreed that Jacob could have Rachael too for a wife, but first he had to celebrate for a week with his new wife Leah. Likewise, Jacob had to work another seven years for Rachael.

Jacob loved Rachael, but he did not have strong feelings for Leah. As a result, God was upset with Jacob because he would not show any love toward Leah. As a result, God blessed Leah with children, but Rachael remained barren for years. As Leah bore sons for Jacob, Rachael became jealous of Leah and angry with Jacob. Finally, after Leah bore six sons and a daughter, God decided to bless Rachael with a son too. This son was name Joseph. When Joseph was born, all his siblings were much older than him. Thus, Jacob considered Joseph a gift from God because he was the child of his old age. This favoritism toward Joseph by Jacob caused resentment and hate within the family, especially among his brothers.

JOSEPH'S DREAMS

We find in the book of Genesis that Joseph's dreams had hidden messages coded with symbolism. Joseph had no idea what the symbolism in his dreams meant. And like all spiritual dreams, they were vivid and powerful. As a result, Joseph wanted to talk about them. Since the symbolism in Joseph's dreams was easy to interpret for his brothers and father, he should have used discretion and not told his family members about his dreams. So by revealing these dreams to his family members, Joseph set in motion a sequence of events that would start his climb to power. A climb to power that would give him authority over his brothers.

There are lessons for us today from Joseph's dreams and his life. The first lesson is that God speaks to us through spiritual dreams that are coded with symbolism. Granted, not all dreams from God are filled with symbolism, but most of them will include symbols that need to be interpreted. The second point is that spiritual dreams are meant for you, not others. In short, be cautious about discussing your spiritual dreams to others because others will not understand your dreams nor believe they are from God. Personally, I've had pastors and strong believers express doubt that my dreams were from God.

Another key point about Joseph's dreams: the meaning of your dream may not be obvious right away. If so, do not get discouraged because in time, God will reveal the meaning of your dream. And like Joseph, you may be too immature spiritually to understand what your dream meant. Therefore, as you grow spiritually, you will understand more about biblical symbols and what they mean. Unfortunately, there is no set template that can accelerate your spiritual growth. A lot will depend on how sincere you are about serving the Lord. There is truth to the adage that "adversity shapes character." Biblical adversity means you have experienced trials and tribulations in life, but kept your faith in God.

In Genesis 41:1–8, we find a dream with symbolic language:

> Then it came to pass, at the end of two full years, that Pharaoh had a dream; and behold, he stood by the river. Suddenly there came up out of the river seven cows, fine looking and fat; and they fed in the meadow. Then behold, seven other cows came up after them out of the river, ugly and gaunt, and stood by the other cows on the bank of the river. And the ugly and gaunt cows ate up the seven fine looking and fat cows. So Pharaoh awoke.

BACKDROP

Joseph was already in prison for years prior to Pharaoh's dreams. He was sent to prison because his master's wife falsely accused him of attacking her. The Lord though blessed Joseph while he was in prison. As a result, he had favor with the keeper of the prison. Because of this favor, the prison keeper granted him authority to watch over the prisoners. This position eventually allowed Joseph to interact with the man who would get him released from prison.

The event that triggered Joseph's release from prison was when Pharaoh got upset with his butler and baker, so he had them thrown into prison—the same one as Joseph. Since Joseph was responsible for the care of all prisoners, Pharaoh's butler and baker were put under his authority as well. One day both men received prophecy dreams from God. They were disturbed by their dreams, but they did not know how to interpret them.

Once Joseph was told about their dreams, he interpreted them. The butler was subsequently restored to his duties after three days; however, the baker was beheaded. Before the butler was released from prison, Joseph requested that he remember him, but the butler failed to do so. Two years later, Pharaoh had his disturbing dreams. When none of Pharaoh's entourage could interpret his dreams, the butler remembered Joseph. Once Joseph met the Pharaoh, he interpreted his dreams. As a result, he became the second most powerful man in Egypt.

Like Joseph, Pharaoh's dreams were filled with symbolism. Matter of fact, most of the spiritual dreams in the Bible are filled with symbolism. God does not tell us in Genesis why he uses symbolism in dreams, but he does so with people of faith and nonbelievers too. In addition, some people are given the gift of dream interpretation such as Joseph.

In Numbers 12:5–6, God reveals how he uses dreams to speak to prophets:

> Then the Lord came down in the pillar of cloud and stood in the door of the tabernacle, and called Aaron and Miriam. And they both went forward. Then he said, "Hear now My words: If there is a prophet among you, I, the Lord, make Myself known to him in a vision; I speak to him in a dream."

The Lord went on to say that Moses is his special servant. Hence, he spoke to him personally rather than through visions or dreams.

The reason the Lord came down to the tabernacle and spoke to Miriam and Aaron was because Moses had married an Ethiopian woman, and they criticized him for doing so. The Bible does not explain why Aaron and Miriam thought this marriage was a bad move. However, in their eyes, they thought they were just as good as Moses because God spoke to them too. The Lord, however, considered Moses the humblest man in the world, so he was quite upset with Aaron and Miriam for belittling his chosen prophet.

BACKDROP

Throughout the Old Testament, God spoke mainly through prophets, not individuals. Thus, if God wanted to convey a message to someone, he would use a prophet to deliver that message. Moses, however, pleased God greatly. So the Lord spoke to him directly. This was a special relationship that no one else in the world had with God at the time. Although the Lord spoke to Aaron and Miriam too, it was because Moses needed help with the tabernacle and the people. But God's relationship with them was not personal. In view of this, when Aaron and Miriam spoke against Moses, they crossed a line with God. And since Miriam was especially critical of Moses, the Lord inflicted her with leprosy. As a result, Moses had to pray for Miriam, and after seven days, the Lord removed her leprosy.

Throughout the Old Testament, most people did not have personal relationships with God, even though that was God's original intent for Adam and Eve. Consequently, after Adam and Eve died, only prophets and priests had direct access to God. Their job was to intercede for the people's sins and receive instructions from God concerning repentance and restitution. Sometimes though, the Lord would send angels to speak to individuals, but most of the people received their spiritual instructions from their priests or prophets. If

God wanted to speak to someone other than a priest or prophet, he would often use dreams to convey that message.

In Joel 2:28–29, we find confirmation that God will use dreams in the last days:

> And it shall come to pass afterward That I will pour out My Spirit on all flesh; Your sons and your daughters shall prophesy, Your old men shall dream dreams, Your young men shall see visions. And also on My menservants and on My maidservants I will pour out My Spirit in those days.

BACKDROP

We know that these verses are about the end times because in Joel 2:30–32, we are told of the events that will follow the awesome day of the Lord. In view of this, what does the reference to "My Spirit" in Joel 2:28–29 represent? The answer is the Holy Spirit. Hence, in the last days, the Holy Spirit will draw many people to Christ. Likewise, those individuals saved during this time will experience higher gifts of the Holy Spirit. Some of these gifts will be spiritual wisdom and knowledge. Furthermore, these gifts will be revealed through dreams and visions. In fact, Joel 2:28–29 is repeated in the book of Acts as confirmation that God will use dreams in the last days to reveal spiritual messages to his people.

The dream message in Joel 2:28–29 concerns prophecy. And when the Bible speaks of prophecy, it's a message concerning future events within one's life or others. Although dreams from God can have many purposes besides prophecy, I believe that if you're experiencing spiritual dreams on a regular basis, you'll find that most of them will be about prophecy coupled with spiritual warfare. You should not dread or fear these dreams. Instead, be thankful that God is preparing you for future events or trials.

In 1 Kings 3:5–9, Solomon is presented the gift of wisdom:

> At Gibeon the Lord appeared to Solomon in a dream by night; and God said, "Ask! What shall I give you?" And Solomon said: "You have shown great mercy to Your servant David my father, because he walked before You in truth, in righteousness, and in uprightness of heart with You; You have continued this great kindness for him, and You have given him a son to sit on his throne, as it is this day. Now, O Lord my God, You have made Your servant king instead of my father David, but I am a little child; I do not know how to go out or come in. And Your servant is in the midst of Your people whom You have chosen, a great people, too numerous to be numbered or counted. Therefore give to Your servant an understanding heart to judge Your people, that I may discern between good and evil. For who is able to judge this great people of Yours?"

BACKDROP

The Lord was greatly please by what Solomon asked for. As a result, he was given the gift of wisdom. This gift of wisdom was supernatural, and no person prior to or after Solomon ever matched his level of wisdom. In addition, God also gave Solomon riches and honor among kings because he was well pleased with him. Solomon achieved a lot for God during the forty years he reigned. A significant achievement was the building of the Temple, which God did not allow David to build because he was a man of war. Unfortunately, when Solomon was old, he allowed himself to be influenced by his foreign wives, and he started worshipping foreign gods.

The dream message of 1 Kings 3:5–9 is about choosing between serving God or self. The Lord told Solomon that if he obeyed his commandants and statutes, his days would be lengthened. Although Solomon did great things for God during his reign, he faltered at the end. Likewise, many people today will have spiritual dreams concerning God's will for their life. God will reveal to them a path that they must follow, and if they follow that path, they will fulfill God's purpose for their life. Like Solomon though, many Christians will serve God enthusiastically for a season, but when pressure comes from the world, flesh, and the enemy, they falter. In view of this, if you have spiritual dreams about following a narrow path, God is telling you not to quit serving him despite all the pressure you're feeling. Remember, you can do all things through Christ, who strengthens you.

In the book of Daniel, we are told about the dreams of Nebuchadnezzar, the king of Babylon. His dreams were about future empires and his own fate due to his arrogance. Nebuchadnezzar was not a man of God; however, he was given a revelation about the future of the world. These dreams disturbed Nebuchadnezzar to such a point that he threatened to kill his wise men unless they could interpret them. None of the Babylonian wise men could cite or interpret the king's dreams, but Daniel could.

In Daniel 1:17, we get an explanation for why God used dreams to convey these messages to Nebuchadnezzar now: "As for these four young men, God gave them knowledge and skill in all literature and wisdom; and Daniel had understanding in all visions and dreams." Daniel's gift of understanding in all visions and dreams would be used by God to promote him and his peers to power in the Babylonian Kingdom.

BACKDROP

The Babylonians has just conquered Jerusalem. And their king, Nebuchadnezzar, decided to select some of the children of Israel to serve in his palace. These individuals had to be good-looking and gifted with wisdom and knowledge. They were to be taught the language and literature of the Chaldeans. Daniel was one of four Jewish children selected to serve the king. In Daniel 2:1–13, we are told about the king's dreams and what he will do if his wise men could not interpret them for him:

> Now in the second year of Nebuchadnezzar's reign, Nebuchadnezzar had dreams; and his spirit was so troubled that his sleep left him. Then the king gave the command to call the magicians, the astrologers, the sorcerers, and the Chaldeans to tell the king his dreams. And the king said to them, "I have had a dream, and my spirit is anxious to know the dream." Then the Chaldeans spoke to the king in Aramaic, "O king, live forever! Tell your servants the dream, and we will give the interpretation." The king answered and said to the Chaldeans, "My decision is firm: If you do not make known the dream to me, and its interpretation, you shall be cut in pieces, and your houses shall be made an ash heap. However, if you tell the dream and its interpretation, you shall receive from me gifts, rewards, and great honor. Therefore, tell me the dream and its interpretation." They answered again and said, "Let the king tell his servants the dream, and we will give its interpretation." The king answered and said, "I know for certain that you would gain time, because you see that my decision is firm: if you do not make known the dream to me, there is only one decree for you! For you have agreed to speak lying and corrupt words before me

> till the time has changed. Therefore tell me the dream, and I shall know that you can give me its interpretation." The Chaldeans answered the king, and said, "There is not a man on earth who can tell the king's matter; therefore no king, lord, or ruler has ever asked such things of any magician, astrologer, or Chaldean. It is a difficult thing that the king requests, and there is no other who can tell it to the king except the gods, whose dwelling is not with flesh." For this reason the king was angry and very furious, and gave the command to destroy all the wise men of Babylon. So the degree went out, and they began killing the wise men; and they sought Daniel and his companions, to kill them.

Daniel subsequently meets with a man name Arioch, who was appointed by the king to kill the wise men. After Daniel persuades Arioch to let him meet with the king, he meets the king and then interprets Nebuchadnezzar's dream. Nebuchadnezzar's dream is perhaps the most famous one in the Bible. This dream is about a great statue. The head of the statue is of gold, the chest and arms are silver, and the belly and thighs are bronze, while the legs are iron and the feet are partly iron and clay.

Daniel goes on to explain that these different parts of the statue represent kingdoms. The current kingdom Babylon is the head of gold. After Babylon falls, the Medes and Persians come to power and are followed by the Greeks, which are followed by the Romans, and in the last days, some form of the Roman Empire will be restored. The final point of Nebuchadnezzar's dream is that God will restore his kingdom, which will never end and be perfect.

These dreams of Nebuchadnezzar were like the ones the Pharaoh of Egypt experienced. In both cases, the most powerful man in the world experienced disturbing dreams from God. Moreover, these rulers were not fearful men. Yet their spiritual dreams from God disturbed them greatly. Likewise, throughout the Bible when one received a dream from God, they knew it was supernatural. Although the ungodly may not have known their dreams were from God, they were powerful and caused these men to search for answers. Thus, God shows us in the Old Testament that spiritual dreams affect people. As a result, they change course.

In 1 Samuel 28:6, we are told about Saul's desperate attempt to hear from the Lord: "And when Saul inquired of the Lord, the Lord did not answer him, either by dreams or by Urim or by the prophets."

BACKDROP

Although this passage is short, it reveals how vivid the Lord's dreams were to Saul. The Bible does not mention how often Saul received messages from God via dreams, but clearly it was often enough that he trusted in them. Saul also depended on Samuel, a prophet, who interceded on his behalf to the Lord; however, Samuel had died by this time. Thus, without Samuel to reassure him and no dreams to ease his fears, Saul panicked because the Philistine Army was preparing to attack Israel.

Saul subsequently resorted to a desperate measure by seeking out a medium in the land. This was considered a great sin in the eyes of the Lord. Once he found a medium at Endor, he convinced her to conduct a séance. Before the woman conducted the ceremony, she asked Saul who he wanted to bring up. He wanted Samuel. Once the séance commenced, the woman saw a sprit that looked like an old man, and Saul perceived it was Samuel. Although Saul was humbled by Samuel's appearance, he quickly became distraught after Samuel spoke these words in 1 Samuel 28:16–19:

> Then Samuel said: "So why do you ask me, seeing the Lord has departed from you and has become your enemy? And the

> Lord has done for Himself as He spoke by me. For the Lord has torn the kingdom out of your hand and given it to your neighbor, David. Because you did not obey the voice of the Lord nor execute His fierce wrath upon Amalek, therefore the Lord has done this thing to you this day. Moreover the Lord will also deliver Israel with you into the hand of the Philistines. And tomorrow you and your sons will be with me. The Lord will also deliver the army of Israel into the hand of the Philistines."

Granted, Saul did not have the Holy Spirit living inside him, which Christians have today. Instead, he had access to God through prophets and dreams. When his access to God was taken away because of his disobedience, he felt lost and afraid. A spiritual dream now would have comforted Saul because he knew it meant that God was with him. Without this assurance from God, fear consumed Saul. This fear led him to desperate measures, which cost him his life.

In Job 33:14–16, we get some insight as to why God uses dreams:

> For God may speak in one way, or in another, Yet man does not perceive it. In a dream, in a vision of the night, When deep sleep falls upon men, While slumbering in their beds, Then He opens the ears of men, And seals their instruction.

BACKDROP

Throughout the book of Job, others expressed their opinions as to why he is suffering. In short, they imply Job is not being honest about his spiritual condition. Thus, God is punishing him for his disobedience. Likewise, Job insists he has done nothing wrong. Conversely, a younger man named Elihu contradicts what Job's friends are saying about the situation. Furthermore, Elihu also disagrees with Job's assessment of the situation. Elihu contends God is God. As such, he is all-powerful, fair, and worthy to be trusted, and no man can proclaim their righteous before him.

The book of Job cites many biblical principles that apply to us today. Although many pastors use the book of Job for sermons on suffering, there are other biblical lessons in Job about God's will, purpose, and his mysterious ways. One of those mysterious ways is mentioned in Job 33:14–16. In short, these verses tell us that God reveals his will in different ways, and one of those ways is through dreams.

For our times, we can conclude from the book of Job that God has a plan. Although Job was never told why he had to suffer, in the end he was blessed because he endured. As Christians, we too will experience hard times that conflict with our belief that God loves us. And when we do experience a period of suffering, God may not reveal the reasons why immediately. In view of this, we must be receptive to hear from God in unconventional ways, and one of those ways is through dreams.

In Matthew 1:20–21, The Angel of the Lord spoke to Joseph:

> But while he thought about these things, behold, an angel of the Lord appeared to him in a dream, saying, "Joseph, son of David, do not be afraid to take to you Mary your wife, for that which is conceived in her is of the Holy Spirit. And she will bring forth a Son, and you shall call His name Jesus, for He will save His people from their sins."

BACKDROP

Joseph by Jewish law was married to Mary; however, they were not allowed to be intimate until after the marriage ceremony. So when Joseph found out that Mary was pregnant, no doubt he was distraught by this development. Despite this perceived betrayal of trust by Mary, Joseph, nevertheless, pondered how to divorce Mary privately. No doubt Joseph loved Mary deeply, but it took a strong level of faith to accept what the Angel of the Lord told him. Likewise, there is no evidence in Scripture that Joseph was upset or tried to argue with the angel about the message.

This was the first spiritual dream recorded in the New Testament. And when you read Matthew 1:20–21, there is no indication Joseph doubted or questioned whether this dream came from God. This dream clearly convinced Joseph not to divorce Mary; moreover, any objections Joseph had concerning Mary as his wife based on Jewish law were never raised. I believe they were not raised because Joseph knew from Old Testament stories that God spoke to people via dreams. So when he experienced his spiritual dream from the Angel of the Lord, he accepted it without question.

In Matthew 2:13–14, the Angel of the Lord spoke to Joseph again to flee to Egypt:

> Now when they had departed, behold an angel of the Lord appeared to Joseph in a dream, saying, "Arise, take the young Child and His mother, flee to Egypt, and stay there until I bring you word; for Herod will seek the young Child to destroy Him." When he arose, he took the young Child and His mother by night and departed for Egypt.

This was the second dream Joseph received from the Angel of the Lord. However, unlike the first dream, this one was a warning concerning a threat to his family along with instructions as to what to do. Joseph did not doubt this dream or its meaning. He immediately acted on it and headed to Egypt. So clearly, Joseph believed this dream without question. And like the first dream he received from God, this one was powerful, vivid, and etched in his memory.

The book of Matthew cites three dreams of Joseph. Although the Bible does not mention whether Joseph had other spiritual dreams, I would contend he probably had many more throughout his lifetime. The proof is in Scripture and based on how Joseph responded to the three dreams cited in the book of Matthew. In all three dreams, he obeyed the instructions given to him. So no doubt when Joseph questioned his role as Jesus earthly father, I believe his dreams from God reassured him.

This assurance from the Lord must have been powerful for Joseph because when Jesus was twelve, he became separated from his family while they visited Jerusalem. After searching for Jesus for three days, they found him in the temple teaching. Jesus does not tell his mother that he is sorry; rather, he simply tells her, "Don't you know that I must do my father's work?" That statement must have troubled Joseph greatly, but there is no mention in the Bible that he became upset or bitter because of it. So clearly, Joseph was given insight about his role as Jesus's father. I believe one aspect of that insight was through dreams.

Joseph's third dream is recorded in Matthew 2:19–22:

> Now when Herod was dead, behold, an angel of the Lord appeared in a dream to Joseph in Egypt, saying, "Arise, take the young Child and His mother, and go to the land of Israel, for those who sought the young Child's life are dead." Then he arose, took the young Child and His mother, and came into the land of Israel.

There are two other dreams of note in the book of Matthew. The first one involved the Three Kings, who visited Jesus. It's recorded in Matthew 2:12: "Then, being divinely warned in a dream that they should not return to Herod, they departed for their own country another way."

The other dream involved Pilate's wife. It's recorded in Matthew 27:19: "While he was sitting on the judgment seat, his wife sent to him, saying, 'Have nothing to do with that just Man, for I have suffered many things today in a dream because of Him.'" The Bible does not provide details of these dreams; however, the Three Kings understood their dream to be a warning not to return to Herod. The dream of Pilate's wife remains a mystery though. Some have suggested that in later years, Pilate's wife became a Christian. The Catholic Church supports this position. In any event, she was clearly disturbed by her dream.

The last dream cited in the New Testament is listed in Act 2:17: "And it shall come to pass in the last days, says God, That I will pour out of My Spirit on all flesh; Your sons and your daughters shall prophesy, Your young men shall see visions, Your old men shall dream dreams." This is the same passage as Joel 2:28–29. The last part of the passage "Your old men shall dream dreams" is a revelation that dreams will be given as a gift in the last days. The fact that old men shall have dreams is not surprising because spiritual dreams from God are filled with symbolism. And to interpret biblical symbolism, you need to know your Bible. Furthermore, the dreams of Acts 2:17 refer to spiritual warfare and how to use the whole armor of God to fight against it.

DREAM FACTOR

If God is using dreams today to convey messages, then it's a factor that can be weighed. If so, how does one determine whether a dream was from God? Based on my experiences with unusual dreams and that of others, I have learned that there are three characteristics of spiritual dreams: The first characteristic will be your emotional response during and after the dream. You will be moved by fear, conviction, or sorrow. The second component of a spiritual dream is the imprint it leaves in your mind. Unlike normal dreams, spiritual dreams are remembered as events you've experienced. The third feature of a spiritual dream is the symbolism within it. A lot of the symbolism within spiritual dreams will have biblical references. For example, you'll have dreams about snakes, chains, wolves, swords, shields, or dark shadows. These symbols represent situations or events you must confront.

Many people in ministry would contend that praying, reading your Bible, and listening to the inner voice of the Holy Spirit is all you need to hear from God. Yet many adults with no Christian backgrounds decide to accept Christ after experiencing a supernatural event. This is especially true for people living in the Third World, where Christians are persecuted.

I contend that dreams are supernatural events that change people. Likewise, dreams can clarify, warn, encourage, and reveal truths to people in ways that cannot be measured. Although spiritual dreams won't always reveal the reasons behind bad events or situations, they can provide closure and peace. Therefore, spiritual dreams are unconventional factors that can reveal tangible reasons for bad events.

Chapter 6

SUFFERING

Many nonbelievers doubt the existence of God because of all the suffering and perceived wrongs in the world. They argue if God is all-powerful, knowing, and loving, why doesn't he do something about the evil in the world? As a Christian, you may try to explain to a nonbeliever about original sin and the consequences for mankind because of it. Likewise, you may try to explain there is evil in the world because of Satan and his demons. And although you know these things to be true based on Scripture, how do you respond when nonbelievers question your faith, character, and reasoning?

If there was ever a person justified to question God and demand answers, it would be Job. We find in Job 1:8 God confirming to Satan about the character of Job: "Then the Lord said to Satan, 'Have you considered My servant Job, that there is none like him on the earth, a blameless and upright man, one who fears God and shuns evil?'" Satan goes on to challenge Job's character. God allows Satan to attack Job. First, Satan destroys Job's family and property, and then he attacks him personally. Job subsequently loses everything, including his reputation and respect among family, friends, and others. And throughout the book of Job, we get commentaries from his friends and others as to why he is suffering. Job insists that he has done nothing wrong, and all his suffering and pain is unjust.

Many of us would think that Job was punished unjustly. As such, God should have commended and comforted Job for enduring all the attacks of Satan and experiencing the harsh ridicule from his friends and others. In fact, we find in Job 38:2–3 that God does just the opposite: "Who is this who darkens counsel By words without knowledge? Now prepare yourself like a man; I will question you, and you shall answer Me." These were the first words God said to Job after everything he just endured. God then reveals his majesty and omnipotence to Job by asking him questions that no man can answer. The point of God's chastisement of Job: who are you to question me?

Many theologians would say the book of Job is about suffering, while other scholars would emphasize the book of Job is about spiritual warfare. One could make a case for either position. I would contend the book of Job is about suffering, spiritual warfare, and us. Although none of us would want to endure what Job did, we all suffer loss in life. I believe another message within the book Job is our response to loss and how it relates to our opinion of God.

Many Christians struggle with the issue of suffering. They struggle with the issue because it's painful to endure and is contrary to how they view love. None of us want to see our children suffer, and it's hard for us to accept that any good can come from watching our children suffer. This is especially true when young children are diagnosed with a serious or terminal condition. Many Christians, therefore, question God when their child or spouse is diagnosed with an incurable disease.

Although our church family and pastor can provide invaluable support during difficult times, sometimes their views on matters are wrong. A great example of this is how Job's friends and family viewed his suffering. Although they were sincere and trying to help Job, they were sincerely wrong concerning Job's suffering. Thus, Job got angry with them and God too. Further, despite Job's constant prayers to God, he was never told why. Yet in the end, Job's reputation and wealth were restored. In view of this, are there lessons we can learn from the book of Job?

The book of Job is a story of faith, endurance, and suffering. Unfortunately, many Christians miss the point of the story. The point is that when we suffer in life, we must be faithful to God. Perhaps in time, God will reveal the reasons for our suffering. If not, the reasons are immaterial. What is material is how we face suffering. Although factors are involved with our suffering, our actions play a role too. Likewise, there are unknown factors that cause us to suffer. Furthermore, we may never know about these factors.

FACTORS

There are many factors to consider about suffering. A major factor is our bodies. With our bodies, we can experience intimacy, love, pleasure, exercise, eating, and drinking. In short, everything that matters can be enjoyed and experienced through our bodies. Yet because of original sin by Adam in the Garden, we are cursed with physical death. And there is nothing pleasurable about the process of dying. Some people die prematurely because of accidents or natural disasters, while many will die from diseases. Even those who die from natural causes will experience some suffering. Since we all die and experience suffering in the process, can God or anyone be blamed for our suffering?

Although it's not a popular subject at the dinner table, everyone knows they will die one day. Most people would like to die at a ripe old age in their sleep. Unfortunately, few get that wish. Instead, barring an accident or terminal disease, most will die slowly as their internal organs slowly shut down. In view of this, does God provide us clues in the Bible about our life span? If so, are there factors that determine how long we live?

In Genesis 6:3, God makes a statement concerning mankind's life span: "And the Lord said, 'My Spirit shall not strive with man forever, for he is indeed flesh; yet his days shall be one hundred and twenty years.'"

Yet a few verses later, God changes in mind about man and decides to destroy him. We find this in Genesis 6:6–7:

> And the Lord was sorry that He had made man on the earth, and He was grieved in His heart. So the Lord said, "I will destroy man whom I have created from the face of the earth, both man and beast, creeping thing and birds of the air, for I am sorry that I have made them."

Despite this, a man name Noah is considered worthy by God to escape the coming flood against mankind. Thus, he is instructed to build an ark. The building of the ark will take 120 years.

Some theologians contend that the 120 years mentioned in Genesis 6:3 refers to the time period for building the ark. Although Noah and his sons lived beyond 120 years, later generations did not. Today, few people live beyond 120 years. Furthermore, Old Testament prophets and Jesus had little to say about life spans. Instead, they cited how disobedience to God can destroy one's body and soul. The one exception in Scripture can be found in Psalm 90:10: "The days of our lives are seventy years; And if by reason of strength they are eighty years, Yet their boast is only labor and sorrow." This psalm refers to the eternity of God and man's frailty. Given this reality, the main point of this verse seems to suggest our days are numbered.

Even today with all our advances in health care and medicine, most people slow down considerably after age seventy. Likewise, many seniors over seventy are either in nursing homes or require extensive medical care and medicine just to live. Sadly, most seniors don't choose to be unhealthy or inactive physically. On the contrary, they would rather be healthy and live productive lives. Unfortunately, there is nothing they can do to stop the aging process. Although people may live longer today, those extra years for many seniors are not productive ones.

Compare modern life spans to those born during biblical times. For example, when Jesus was born, most people died before reaching forty. Furthermore, the book of Psalms was written hundreds of years prior to the birth of Christ. So where did the writer of Psalm 90:10 get his information that productive lives decline after age seventy? Because based on what we know about ancient life spans, few people lived to be seventy, much less eighty. In view of this, what is the writer telling us in Psalm 90:10?

I believe this psalm concerns our life span and what we do with it. In addition, I believe the seventy years is a time frame to evaluate what we did with our lives. Thus, we either lived a life that pleased God, or we lived for pleasure and gain. Furthermore, the healthiest period of our lives is the first seventy years. After that, the aging process accelerates, and our ability to achieve things physically and mentally are limited. We find verses in Ecclesiastes chapter 3 that cite a season or time for everything. Hence, is seventy years one of those times?

As our body dies, we will experience frustration, fear, anger, and regrets from our past. Although everyone would like to make amends for past mistakes, debating hindsight will only cause depression. In the end, your relationship with God will determine how you face suffering and death. Although God's power is beyond our comprehension, even faithful servants will experience sorrow and disappointments in life. What matters is how we finish our Christian journey because life is a race against time. This is outlined in James 4:14–15:

> Whereas you do not know what will happen tomorrow. For what is your life? It is even a vapor that appears for a little time and then vanishes away. Instead you ought to say, "If the Lord wills, we shall live and do this or that."

Despite what some churches teach today about God's prosperity, the Christian life is difficult, long, and frustrating. Nevertheless, all faithful Christians know the Lord walked with them during difficult times. The Bible states that Christians will have trouble in the world. Conversely, Jesus tells us he has overcome the world. Thus, true peace of mind can only occur when one accepts these two biblical truths. Yes, it hurts when our bodies and minds decline. However, our human body was never meant to be permanent. It's simply the body we occupy in this world. In view of this, one should never blame God when their physical health declines. Instead, call upon God to provide the grace needed to be faithful to the end. Because in many ways, how you finish your life matters to those who knew you.

Wound Factors

All Christians have experienced hurt from people they love and know. Often our parents, siblings, children, spouses, and friends caused these hurts. In time though, we're able to forgive and move on from past hurts. Still, many Christians won't forgive and release past wrongs, mainly because the offense caused deep psychological and emotional pain. A good example of this is the sexual abuse many girls experienced in their home from a father figure or sibling. Unfortunately, even after a Christian woman forgives the person who violated them, they are unable to release the emotional pain caused by the offense.

Christians have an adversary that does not play by the rules. That adversary is Satan. In John 10:10, we're warned about Satan and his plan of attack: "The thief does not come except to steal, and to kill, and to destroy. I have come that they may have life, and that they may have it more abundantly." This passage is short and to the point. In view of this, Christians must recognize that Satan uses past emotional wounds to hinder their spiritual growth. Furthermore, these past emotional wounds are crippling believers spiritually. As a result, many faithful Christians suffer in life, and they don't understand why.

Although sexual offenses are extremely difficult to confess and release, other common hurts can be confronted and removed almost immediately. For example, the emotional wound caused by divorce has profoundly affected the Church. Although many Christian children of divorce will eventually forgive their parents, they fail to release the hurt associated with it. As a result, they may experience marital strife in their marriage too, and they won't understand why. As a result, they blame their spouse for the strife, when in fact, they have unrealistic expectations for their marriage. Further, any confrontation with their spouse relating to marital problems will often trigger bad childhood memories. Therefore, recognizing and confessing emotional hurt caused by a divorce is the only way for spiritual healing to take place.

Whether one is a child of divorce, sexual abuse, or has experienced some other emotional wounds from their past, there are three levels of forgiveness and release that must be followed: a mental, emotional, and spiritual component. To release a wrong mentally simply means you no longer think about the wrong. An emotional release simply means the pain of the wrong no longer upsets you. To release a matter spiritually requires forgiveness toward the individual who wronged you, even if that person is deceased.

In addition, you must acknowledge and ask God to remove these hurts from your soul. This is necessary because your soul has been wounded. Thus, to heal your soul, all three components of the hurt must be addressed. If not, the wound will not heal. In Hebrews 12:15, we are warned about bitterness and unforgiveness: "Looking carefully lest anyone fall short of the grace of God; lest any root of bitterness springing up cause trouble, and by this many become defiled." The devil knows this verse well, and it's his right to torment you concerning past wrongs if bitterness is not released.

THE WOMAN FACTOR

Women understand and are more open about addressing past wounds than men, while many men will not address or admit their emotional wounds unless they experience a traumatic event such as PTSD (post-traumatic stress disorder) after serving in combat. Unfortunately, many veterans refuse to address their PTSD condition. Instead, they would rather isolate themselves and not confront their emotional wound. In fact, they need counseling and the support of loved ones to address their emotional wounds.

Most men do not suffer from PTSD; however, many have experienced wounds from their past. Yet many men neither understand their past wounds, nor do they know how to heal them. Women, however, can see their wounds clearly. In 1 Peter 3:7, husbands are given a word about wives: "Husbands, likewise, dwell with them with understanding, giving honor to the wife, as to the weaker vessel, and as being heirs together of the grace of life, that your prayers may not be hindered." The words *weaker vessel* is not a negative remark. Instead, I believe it refers to the emotional and psychological makeup of women. In short, they feel more deeply than men, they express emotion more deeply than men, and they have unique skills for understanding and maintaining relationships.

Since women have excellent communication skills, they can encourage men to seek help for their problems. Still, how that support is presented makes all the difference. For example, the love and support of a Christian wife can convict a husband to get better. Conversely, a nagging and contentious wife can create anger and resentment. Although many times men cannot see or understand their problems clearly, they still want to be respected by their wives.

In Proverbs 21:19, the writer expresses a timeless message that still resonates with men today: "Better to dwell in the wilderness, than with a contentious and angry woman." Unfortunately, many women have become bitter and contentious because of emotional wounds from men they loved and tried to help.

A powerful tenet that is expressed throughout the Bible is knowledge. The phrase *lack of knowledge* is mentioned many times in Scripture. The word *knowledge* is referring to the ways of God. In short, if one does not know the ways of God for handling situations, mistakes can be made that cause hardship and spiritual separation from God. Unfortunately, although Christians today have tremendous resources for understanding and applying God's Word to situations, many times they do not use these resources. Instead, they rely on worldly solutions to address spiritual problems.

No doubt emotional wounds caused by family and others are spiritual scars that must be addressed through forgiveness. Yet they are the hardest ones to release. Many Christian women suffer because of the scars caused by their fathers and men who hurt them, whereas men have been scarred due to the neglect of their fathers. In view of this, the Church cannot be politically correct regarding the roles and responsibilities of men. Boys need the interaction and support of their fathers while little girls need to be loved and approved by their fathers. When children do not get the attention needed from their fathers, this will affect their emotional and spiritual health.

In Matthew 7:7, we are given instructions for praying: "Ask, and it will be given to you; seek, and you will find; knock, and it will be opened to you." This verse is Jesus's instructions for us when praying. If so, why do we have unanswered prayers? One reason is unforgiveness and bitterness toward our parents and others who have hurt us. In addition, we may not be consciously aware of the hurt they caused us. In view of this, if you continue to have relationship issues with your spouse or others, ask the Lord for discernment. Conversely, if you know there are issues with your parents, as a Christian, you must forgive and let it go, even if that parent won't acknowledge the wrong against you. It's not your job to correct or demand restitution from them—that is God's job!

On a personal note, when I retired from the US Army, I experienced the loss of my career and family within a few years. When I subsequently remarried, I started to experience uncontrolled anger that consumed me. The anger was so bad, I had to move out. The Lord knew why I moved out. As a result, I was given insight concerning my anger. One night, I woke up with sharp pain in my chest. The pain was so severe that I could barely breathe. I knew this pain was not a heart attack. Instead, I knew this was the emotional pain I held through the years from all the people who hurt me. Likewise, the Holy Spirit told me to forgive all the people who hurt me through the years. I did, and the pain left. Granted, there were other factors to my anger that needed to be addressed besides emotional scars, but my wounds caused by people had to be confessed and released first.

Many faithful Christians suffer emotionally because of past wrongs. Granted, these wounds may have been horrendous. Nevertheless, God says to forgive. In addition, you must release the emotional and spiritual wounds. No, there is no ten-step program to do this psychologically. Instead, this is a spiritual matter that must be addressed by God. Even if you don't understand the reasons for your suffering, God knows. Sometimes the issue will have an emotional, psychological, physical, and spiritual component to it. Each area will have to be addressed. Although God can heal you instantly, he wants his children to work through their problems by relying on him and his Word.

SUMMATION

The Bible says that our life is but a vapor—it's short, and then we're gone. We live in a fallen world with bodies that decay. Our body will weaken as we get older based on many factors. Our diet, exercise, level of stress, hereditary, and spiritual conditions all contribute to how long we live and the quality of that life. Some of us inherited genetic conditions that may end our life prematurely despite how healthy we live. Conversely, some of us were born with healthy bodies with good genetics, but choose to abuse our body with drugs, alcohol, and unhealthy foods. So how we live with the bodies given to us is a matter of faith. Some of us will not live long by today's standards, while others will live long and have many physical ailments to deal with daily. Hence, regardless of the health of your body and length of your life, nowhere in Scripture does God promise you a pain-free life. Instead, we're told that God is with you through the peaks and valleys of your life.

Many believers suffer in life because of physical ailments. Unfortunately, based on false theology and wrong thinking, many Christians blame God when they get diagnosed with a serious ailment. Yet the root causes for many serious or terminal diseases have measurable factors that can be calculated. For example, genetic, environmental, eating and drinking habits, and substance abuse factors can all cause physical ailments—some of which are terminal. If there are cause-and-effect laws for known factors that can cause physical ailments, why do Christians blame God?

Despite measurable factors that can cause physical ailments, *God may intervene supernatural and spare one's life despite their terminal condition.* So why does God spare one cancer victim, but allow many more to die? Did God love that individual more than the rest? The short answer is no. Scripture tells us that God is not a respecter of persons. Thus, if one is Born Again, they have equal access to God to ask for divine healing. In view of this, if God decides not to spare one from their fate, do we concede that that is his Will? In Isaiah 55:8–9, we are told why God can be trusted:

> "For My thoughts are not your thoughts, Nor are your ways My ways," says the Lord. "For as the heavens are higher than the earth, So are My ways higher than your ways, And My thoughts than your thoughts."

Unlike physical ailments, emotional wounds require Christians to forgive and release their hurts. Although it's easy to say, the process of emotional and spiritual healing takes time. Unfortunately, many of these wounds are deep and go back to one's childhood. Likewise, often these hurts get reopened due to words or actions by others. As a result, many people develop coping mechanisms to protect themselves. Often these coping mechanisms involve substance abuse. Sadly, many Christians follow this pattern too. In the end, Christians who never learn how to forgive and release painful wounds rob themselves of joy in this life. Furthermore, they never accomplish God's purpose for them.

No doubt, physical ailments and emotional wounds are difficult issues to reconcile with God. Yet God did not cause your physical or emotional wounds. Yes, God has the power to heal all wounds, but he will never overrule your free will. So if your free will holds on to grudges, dislikes, and unforgiveness toward others, this will hinder God's ability to heal you. God is holy. Thus, he cannot operate against his principles and laws.

Like Job, we cannot argue or present a case to God that justifies our anger, bitterness, and unforgiveness toward others. Granted, the natural man (unsaved person) does not have the ability to forgive and release wrongs. But the spiritual man can act like God. Once a Christian understands this truth, they can release their suffering.

Chapter 7

FINAL THOUGHTS

One reason older people love to be around children is because they view things simply. In short, the way children ask questions and see things is straightforward. They are neither disingenuous or rude, but honest in how they see things. Granted, as they get older, they learn to say things differently. Nevertheless, most kids will give you an honest answer that many adults won't. Furthermore, children believe in things more deeply than adults. Although many of the things they believe in such as Santa Claus, the Tooth Fairy, or Easter Bunny are not real—they are to them. Unfortunately, when they learn there is no Santa, Fairy, or Easter Bunny, they lose part of their innocence.

Many adults long for that childlike faith they once had in imaginary characters or people. Adults long for this innocence because life has been difficult and hurtful. As a result, they have lost faith in people, institutions, and God. Granted, people are imperfect and will let you down. Likewise, both private and governmental agencies don't always do the right things. And sometimes, those wrong actions affect you directly. In time though, many people accept and understand why others and organizations let them down. Still, often their anger and disappointment with God does not subside.

When Jesus's disciples were questioning him about who was greatest in the kingdom of heaven, they expected him to cite the great prophets of the Old Testament. Instead, Jesus pointed to a child. In Matthew 18:2–4, we get Jesus's reply:

> Then Jesus called a little child to Him, set him in the midst of them, and said, "Assuredly, I say to you, unless you are converted become as little children, you will by no means enter the kingdom of heaven." Therefore whoever humbles himself as this little child is the greatest in the kingdom of heaven.

No doubt Jesus is referring to how children believe in things and people unconditionally. Jesus's point to his disciples: you must have fanatical faith in God that cannot be shaken.

In view of this, Christians must forgive and extend grace to others and not hold grudges toward God. Yes, you've been hurt, and no one has the right to dismiss or belittle your pain and disappointments in life. And frankly, only God can truly understand your pain. Likewise, only God can truly remove it from your soul. Yet the process of believing and letting God heal you is a matter of trust. So do you truly trust God? Unfortunately, many Christians have never learned to trust God unconditionally. Yes, they are saved, but they don't have an intimate relationship with God.

When I recruited for the army, I would tell teenagers that the way they think now would change as they got older. My sales pitch: the way you think now is not the way you will think at twenty-one. And the way you think at twenty-one won't be the way you think at twenty-five. Point: your life and viewpoint changes as you mature and gain experience. This applies to our Christian journey too. God never promised you a rose garden. What he promised you was his presence and peace. In John 16:33, Jesus confirms this: "These things I have spoken to you, that in Me you may have peace. In the world you will have tribulation; but be of good cheer, I have overcome the world."

BAD THINGS HAPPEN

The thesis of this book is that bad things happen because of factors. Although there are many factors to ponder when something bad happens in the world or to us, there are only three categories that matter: God, Satan, and random chance. These three categories have many tentacles that may intertwine. Seldom can one cite only God, the devil, or something else when a bad event occurred. Yes, we want answers when bad things happen—especially when bad things happen to us or loved ones. Despite this desire to know why, we may never know why a bad event occurred.

If you are a Christian, you must concede all doubts, worries, and fears to God. Because if you believe that God exists, then he is beyond your understanding. Our minds cannot fully comprehend the majesty of God. If God created the universe, then we are like insects compared to him. Yet he loves those who love him. Based on this spiritual tenet, how can anyone question him? No doubt there are reasons why God allows Christians to suffer. Nevertheless, it's not our job to determine why. If we are walking in faith daily, God promises to take care of us, even if that care is to be with us as we utter our last breath.

Conversely, as a Christian, you must concede we have an adversary. That adversary is Satan. I don't think most Christians realize how much Satan hates mankind. Thus, whether you want to ponder it or not, he hates you! Likewise, I don't think many Christians realize the extent of Satan's evil in the world. He and his demons are responsible for many of the unspeakable evil acts committed in the world, directly or indirectly. In view of this, even though the Church is divided over biblical doctrine, acknowledging Satan as our principal adversary is a tenet that all Christians must agree upon. Jesus tells us clearly in John 10:10 Satan's role and how to overcome his attacks: "The thief does not come except to steal, and to kill, and to destroy. I have come that they may have life, and that they may have it more abundantly."

Although Satan is responsible for many bad things in the world, he cannot be blamed for everything. Satan is not everywhere, nor does he have unlimited power. In view of this, sometimes bad events occur because of random chance. For example, the collapse of a bridge, an automobile accident, or physical injuries while exercising or at work can all occur without outside influences involved. In addition, many of the bad things Christians experience simply happen due to random chance. Likewise, many devastating storms and natural disasters are not caused by God or the devil. Instead, they are caused by atmospheric factors that cannot be controlled by man.

Bad things also occur because of random chance, and believers and nonbelievers will experience these events in their lives. In addition, God and the devil uses these events for their purposes. God will use these events to build faith and trust in him, whereas Satan uses these events to create anger and bitterness toward God. So again, this comes down to your faith and trust in God. The Bible says that faith is the substance of things hoped for and the evidence of things not seen. When you can view faith in this light, nothing on earth or beneath it can separate you from God's loving arms.

SALVATION VERSES

> For God so loved the world that He gave His only begotten Son, that whoever believes in Him should not perish but have everlasting life.
>
> —(John 3:16)
>
> That if you confess with mouth the Lord Jesus and believe in your heart that God has raised Him from the dead,
>
> you will be saved. For with the heart one believes unto righteous, and with the mouth confession is made unto salvation.

—(Rom. 10:9-10)

> For the wages of sin is death, but the gift of God is eternal life in Christ Jesus our Lord.

—(Rom. 6:23)

> Jesus answered and said to him, "Most assuredly, I say to you, unless one is born again, he cannot see the kingdom of God."

—(John 3:3)

> Not everyone who says to Me, "Lord, Lord," shall enter the kingdom of heaven, but he who does the will of My Father in heaven.

—(Matt. 7:21)

> I am the door. If anyone enters by Me, he will be saved, and will go in and out and find pasture.

—(John 10:9)

> Jesus said to him, "I am the way, the truth, and the life. No one comes to the Father except through Me."

—(John 14:6)

SCRIPTURE

The verses of the Bible are powerful if you know how to apply them to situations. No verse in the Bible is more powerful than another—it's all God's Word. Every Christian has their favorite verses they cite or dwell on during difficult times. I have found that the following verses can apply to any spiritual situation:

Which of you by worrying can add one cubit to his statue?

—(Matt. 6:27)

Therefore do not worry, saying, "What shall we eat?" or "What shall we drink?" or "What shall we wear?" For after all these things the Gentiles seek. For your heavenly Father knows that you need all these things. But seek first the kingdom of God and His righteousness, and all these things shall be added to you.

—(Matt. 6:31–33)

Ask, and it will be given to you; seek, and you will find; knock, and it will be opened to you.

—(Matt. 7:7)

Come to Me, all you who labor and are heavy laden, and I will give you rest. Take My yoke upon you and learn from Me, for I am gentle and lowly in heart, and you will find rest for Your souls. For My yoke is easy and My burden is light.

—(Matt. 11:28–30)

And we know that all things work together for good to those who love God, to those who are called according to His purpose.

—(Rom. 8:28)

For I am persuaded that neither death nor life, nor angels nor principalities nor powers, nor things present nor things to come, nor height nor depth, nor any other created thing, shall be able to separate us from the love of God which is in Christ Jesus our Lord.

—(Rom. 8:38–39)

Be anxious for nothing, but in everything by prayer and supplication, with thanksgiving, let your requests be made known to God; and the peace of God, which surpasses all understanding, will guard your hearts and minds through Christ Jesus.

—(Phil. 4:6–7)

For God has not given us a spirit of fear, but of power and of love and of a sound mind.

—(2 Tim. 1:7)

Therefore submit to God. Resist the devil and he will flee from you.

—(James 4:7)

The steps of a good man are ordered by the Lord, And He delights in his way.

—(Ps. 37:23)

Cast your burden on the Lord, And He shall sustain you; He shall never permit the righteous to be moved.

—(Ps. 55:22)